The Life and Times of Jimmy Mullins

and Other Stories

Mary Rose Tobin

First Published 2024
Frank Fahy Publishing Services
5 Village Centre
Barna, Galway
Ireland
www.write-on.ie

All characters and events in this publication, other than those clearly in the public domain, are fictitious, and any resemblance to persons living or dead is purely coincidental.
© 2024 Mary Rose Tobin
Cover photograph: *The Rose* © 2024 Professor Chaosheng Zhang, University of Galway

ISBN: 9798874185039
Imprint: Independently published by Fahy Publishing Services, Barna, Galway.

The Write-on Group wish to thank Galway County Council for helping to fund our various publications and activities.

Comhairle Chontae na Gaillimhe
Galway County Council

The moral right of the author has been asserted. No part of this publication may be reproduced, stored in a retrieval system, or transmitted in any form, or by any means without the prior permission in writing of the Publisher. The views expressed by the author are not necessarily the views of the Publisher.

DEDICATION

To Frank Fahy, for his unfailing support and relentless pursuit of excellence in both writing and editing. Your commitment to the craft has been the cornerstone of this journey.

And to the Write-on Group, whose constant encouragement and camaraderie have been a source of inspiration and motivation. Your unwavering belief in the power of words and stories has been instrumental in bringing this collection to life.

It shows how believing in oneself and having a supportive community can make storytelling magical.

CONTENTS

Introduction vi

A Busy Morning 3

The Intrusion 7

Dear Da 9

Santa's Secret 13

The Dead Language Teacher 17

Getting on with Act Three 33

The Redbridge Show 37

Faraway Hills 43

Evie's First Job 53

The Real Africa 65

Another Mouth to Feed 71

The Secret 77

Mr Boopathy 83

Arise! 95

Lift Up Your Heads 99

The Audition 107

Chance Encounters 115

Les Amants d'un Jour 131

Seville Oranges 135

Hijacked 145

Best Served Cold 149

The Mizpah Ring 163

The Magic of Believing 169

Winner of the 2023 Siarscéal Hanna Greally International Short Story Competition 175

The Life and Times of Jimmy Mullins 177

About the Author 187

Introduction

With this collection, I invite readers on a journey through time and space, from the narrow streets of Galway to the far reaches of Africa and India, to Victorian London and into the intimate corners of human experiences. These stories, crafted over six years as a member of the Galway Write-on Group, are close reflections of life's complexities, joys, and sorrows.

Our voyage begins with **Galway Memories**, stories set against the backdrop of my beloved hometown. From the contrasting lives of children in *The Intrusion* to the adolescent high jinks in *The Dead Language Teacher*, these stories are windows into Galway's past, revealing the city's transformation over the decades. They are not just recollections; they are remnants of an Old Galway that is still etched deeply in my heart.

The narrative shifts to present times, exploring the evolving Irish society and the enduring charm of **Rural Life.** *Getting on with Act Three; The Redbridge Show;* and *Faraway Hills* present contemporary challenges and traditional values, reflecting the diverse facets of Irish life today.

Evie's First Job delves into the universal rite of passage into the **Working World**, while **International Adventures** take us on a journey beyond Irish shores. From the vibrant streets of India in *Mr Boopathy* to the potholed roads of Zambia, these stories transcend boundaries, showcasing the richness of diverse cultures and experiences. The African tales are particularly close to my heart, born from my experiences and observations on that continent. These stories, including *The Real Africa, Another Mouth to Feed* and *The Secret*, are an attempt to capture the essence of a land so vibrant and yet so misunderstood, telling tales of its people, its challenges, and its unyielding spirit.

Adding to this rich collection are **The Foundlings** – four stories about Lucy, a foundling girl navigating the challenges of Victorian London. In *Arise!; Lift Up Your Heads; The Audition;* and *Chance Encounters,* we follow Lucy's journey of resilience and discovery in a world where her beginnings define her less than her dreams.

The stories in the final section are narratives that transcend geographical locations, focusing instead on the universal themes of **Love, Friendship, Revenge, and Growth**. These are stories that resonate with everyone, anywhere, reminding us of our shared humanity. The book concludes with my award winning story – *The Life and Times of Jimmy Mullins.*

Each story in this collection is a piece of a larger puzzle, representing the varied aspects of life and the richness of different cultures. They are tales of the past and present, near and far, but all are deeply human at their core. As you turn these pages, I hope you find pieces of yourself in these stories, as I have found pieces of myself in writing them.

Mary Rose Tobin
January 2024

Galway Memories

A Busy Morning

The little girl had a lot to do. The morning couldn't be long enough.

'Keep an eye on Michael in his pram,' her mother had ordered, 'and run straight in to tell me if he cries.'

But how could she stay in the garden with so much else going on outside?

Two big pillars framed the gate. She clambered up to sit on top of one. Sandaled feet dangling, bare legs scratching against the stippled concrete, she made a list in her head.

First, she had to have her daily chat with the students as they made their leisurely way along Canal Road to the university.

The little girl always had some important news to tell them as they passed.

'We're getting a new baby!'

'We're having lamb for our dinner!'

Today's news was delivered very urgently. 'Look at our poster! We're having a play on Saturday. At three o'clock. We made a stage in the garage.'

Lots of them looked at the poster and said they'd love to come. They were nearly grown-ups, so they didn't mind paying 2d to get in. Those who hesitated were soon persuaded when they heard about the free ice-pop at the interval.

Now, she had to tend to the snails. There were four of them in the race, making their way up the huge wooden telephone pole just to the left of the gate. Her mother owned the grey one; Daddy, the brown speckled one; then Michael had one, but he couldn't talk so that didn't matter; and hers was the biggest but also the slowest. They were still a long way from the poster, which was the finishing line. Actually, she didn't think any of them had budged since yesterday. She retrieved a cabbage leaf from the pocket of her summer dress. One of her student friends told her cabbage would make the snails go faster. Prising out the drawing pin, she replaced the old cabbage leaf with the new.

Then, she turned her attention to the swans. She crossed the road and stuck her head in between the canal's iron railings. Her pigtail got caught in the middle railing and as she jerked her head away, she saw her yellow ribbon flutter into the canal – like a butterfly, she thought. Good riddance!

And there they were, the big white swans – the daddy swan was called Pen, her mother told her, and the mammy swan was named Cob. And the six grey baby swans were all called Signal.

'Here Poll, Poll, Poll,' she entreated. This was what you called swans, even though it wasn't their names. The Signals looked her way, but Pen and Cob ignored her.

She knew how to cut through their indifference. Running back across the road, she fell to her knees on the grass verge. The digging spot. The little trowel was there since before. She dug deep to unearth fresh, moist clay. In no time at all, large, pink, wriggly worms presented themselves in a squirming mass. She managed to

A Busy Morning

catch four, plump and juicy. She knew a way to make them last.

Folding up her skirt, she popped them into her lap. 'You need to get two days out of that dress,' her mother had said earlier. 'Please don't get it all muddy again.' Maybe she would be too busy to notice.

Now she was on her hunkers back by the railings, enthusiastically chopping the worms in half, with the sharp edge of the trowel. Daddy told her that worms didn't have any feelings. Soon, she would have eight live pieces for Pen and Cob and the babies. She delayed for a moment because she loved watching the two halves wriggling off in opposite directions.

Engrossed in her task, she failed to notice the big boy and his sister until they were almost on top of her. They stopped to watch. They didn't understand that the worms had to feed all the swans even though she did her best to explain.

'You're a wicked little girl,' the big boy said.

'Yes,' his sister agreed. 'You'll go to Hell for doing that!'

The little girl ran crying into the kitchen where her mother was peeling potatoes and carrots.

'What is it, love?' the mother asked, absently. 'Is Michael crying?'

'No, no, he's not crying, but they told me I'd go to Hell.'

The mother wiped her hands on her apron. She lifted the little girl up onto the draining board.

'Now, what's all this about Hell? Who told you that? What were you doing?' the mother's rapid-fire questions were delivered in a soft, comforting voice.

'I was only cutting up the worms. I was making sure that there would be plenty to feed to the swans. But what's Hell?'

'Never you mind about Hell,' said the mother, her face reddening. 'If I catch the blackguards who said that to you, they'll feel the back of my hand. Who are they? Tell me their names.'

'John Winters, and Marian.'

'Well, that explains it. Don't mind anything they say, they're only Protestants!'

The mother hoisted the little girl into her arms.

'Oh, look at that dress,' she said. 'I only put it on you clean this morning!'

The little girl knew that her mother wasn't that cross with her.

'Here, pet, take this with you and off you go.' She handed a washed, peeled carrot to the child.

Feeling happier, the girl bit into the carrot and raced back outside to finish feeding the swans. Soon, it would be time to sit back up on the pillar again and watch out for Daddy's car.

The Intrusion

The sun shone on the scene in the back garden. Sitting on the grass in the shade of the apple tree, the little girl studied the array of dolls and teddy bears spread out on the rug before her. Every toy had a role to play. The child was an earnest conductor.

Without warning, a boy came crashing through the side gate, breathing hard. Instinctively, the girl absorbed every detail, even though she could only see up to the middle of his chest. Blue shirt. Red tie. Short trousers. Knee socks. Heavy boots. But her attention was drawn to his arm. It was in a sling.

He skidded to a momentary halt before shooting in under the thick privet hedge.

Before the child had time to contemplate this mystery, a further pair of legs pounded into the garden and intruded at her eye level. A large man. Panting. He stopped in front of the hedge. Wordlessly, he hauled the boy from his hiding place and frog-marched him away. In an instant, they were gone.

'What happened?' the little girl asked her mother. 'Who were they?'

The mother hesitated before replying. 'Don't worry, love, that boy was just a runaway from St Jude's.'

'What's a runaway? What happened to his arm? And what will happen now?'

Mary Rose Tobin

    The mother sighed. 'Come on inside, pet. Forget about all that now. It's time for your tea.'
    The little girl jumped from the rug to follow her mother inside. 'Can we have ice-cream after tea?'

Dear Da

Sunday, 14 November 1954

Dear Da,
I am writing to tell you that I am in a lot of trouble at school and Ma said I had to write to you to tell you what's going on. I wish you lived here with us instead of in London. You would be able to help me. Ma says I'm seven now, and I should be able to look out for myself and anyway, it doesn't matter what Canon Moloney says cause he's only an auld rip. Johnny and Peter want to go down to the nun to talk to her, but Ma won't let them.

It's been bad now for a while, Da. I went into the First Communion class in September after you went back to London from your holidays. It's very hard, Da, and there's an awful lot of catechism and my book is in a state, but Ma says it was good enough for the four before me and it will be good enough for the three after me. I sit beside a nice girl, Da, Jennifer, and she always knows her catechism. She's real nice, Da, there's a lovely smell off her and her hair is really shiny, and she has lovely Clarke's sandals. She was looking at my jelly sandals one day and she even said she'd like to have them, but I know hers are better and my feet are all blue in mine. When I'm big I will always have Clarke's sandals and socks of my own.

You know I have to get in early, Da, for the cocoa-and-bread-and-dripping in the morning. Ma is always saying don't be making a beggar of myself but sometimes it's so cold and the cocoa really warms me up. Some days Ma keeps me home from school until the rain stops and some days, she doesn't let me go at all. She says she won't let me catch my deathacold going down to them bitchesanuns in the Presentation. I don't mind the rain, Da, I just run down Prospect Hill to the Square and on past the Franciscans to the old jail and sure when I'm passing the Poor Clare's, I'm nearly there. But every time I miss a day, the nun catches me by the shoulders and shakes me and says to tell my mammy I'm not a sugar lump and I'll never make anything of myself unless I come to school.

Da, I figured out a way to learn the catechism questions. I sit in the third row beside Jennifer. The girls in the first two rows are always asked before us. So, Jennifer gets the fifth question and I get the sixth one. When I'm learning my catechism homework, I find a place to sit in the kitchen and read the sixth question over and over until I know it off by heart. Ma wants me to help with the small ones, and the lads are always horsing around, but I just learn the question first and don't do anything else until I know it.

Sometimes the nun even says something nice to me like: 'you're not much good at anything else but at least you learn your catechism'. So, it was all going well until last week. On Monday I got to school and there was no sign of Jennifer. We all sat down after the cocoa and the nun told us Jennifer wouldn't be in today because her granny died. That was all right, even though it was sad, but when it came to the catechism, I ended up getting the fifth question. That day, I was in the corner until going-home time.

The next day, Jennifer was back. That day, I knew two questions, but it nearly killed me learning them there was so much going on at home. When we all sat down after the prayer, the nun told us about Jennifer's granny and she was so nice to Jennifer, calling her a poor little chicken and asking after her mammy and even though I like Jennifer, I had a horrible feeling because the nun was so nice to her and so mean to me all the time.

That day passed and I knew my question, and the next day, it was pouring rain and Ma wouldn't let me down to them bitchesanuns to catch my deathacold so I stayed at home and helped get the dinner and wash up and we did a bit of darning.

The real trouble began the next day. I ran like the wind into school. The sun was shining, I knew my question and I had no worries. But when the nun gave me the cocoa, she said to me: 'And where were you yesterday, Miss?' I hate being called Miss, Da, so I knew I was in for a shaking and a telling off. I had a bright idea. Jennifer didn't get into any trouble when she missed a day. 'I couldn't come in, Sister. My Granny died'.

The nun's face changed, and a soft expression came over her face. 'Which Granny died, loveen?' she said with a kind look. 'Your Ma's mother or your Da's?'

I had to think quickly.

'My Da's mother,' I said.

'Oh', she said. 'Poor Mrs McMahon. All the nuns were so fond of her. We'll visit the house this very evening.'

On Friday when I got to school there was no kind look on the nun's face. She caught me by the shoulders and shook me until my teeth rattled. 'You wicked, wicked child,' she said. 'The Reverend Mother and I went over to Canal Road last night to sympathise with your family – and your dead Granny answered the door.' Her voice got louder and louder as she screamed: 'We're sending you to Canon Moloney and he will decide how to punish you.'

I was horrified, Da. When Jennifer said her Granny died, everybody was so nice to her. Anyway, that's why Ma said I had to write to you because of having to see Canon Moloney next week and disgracing the family and giving them bitchesanuns more to gossip about.

That's it, Da. I wish you lived here with us instead of in London and maybe you could go and beat up Canon Moloney and the main thing is I miss you and I didn't mean it.

*From your loving daughter,
Annie*

Santa's Secret

The little girl loved her Daddy more than anyone else in the world. He loved her too, she knew. He didn't tell her in so many words, but he picked her up and swung her around, sang songs to her and told her special stories. He helped her with her homework and, some nights, when he wasn't tired, he put her to bed. Those were her favourite times, when he said her prayers with her, making a joke of them and warning her not to tell her mother. No need for the warning; she'd never tell on her Daddy. She knew he preferred her to her little brothers and sisters, probably because she got there before them.

'How's my first-born?' he would enquire when he came home in the evenings.

If Daddy was tired it was different. Sometimes he came home from work with a peculiar smell and his face looked funny, especially his eyes. On those occasions, being tired made him cross. Everyone had to go to bed quickly and quietly. Mum's face got sad. If you sneaked out and listened at the bannisters, you might hear loud voices downstairs that gave you a strange feeling in your stomach. These things happened when he was bad tired.

But there was good tired too – nights when Daddy would bring sweets home. He would tell everyone they could stay up past their bedtime. He would listen to records, and the children would all join in and sing with him. Sometimes they would dance. All except Mum. She always just wanted him to have his tea and go to bed.

The little girl was eight now and she was so looking forward to Christmas. Everyone, even Daddy, helped to put the tree up. The house looked like a fairy kingdom with all the tinsel and decorations. And she had been so good – helping Mum any time she was asked and being kind to her brothers and sisters. Santa would definitely come this year and bring her everything she asked for in the letter she posted up the chimney all those weeks ago.

She hoped and hoped Daddy would not be tired when he got home. But as soon as he turned the key in the front door, she knew that he was. And it was bad tired.

She was on the sitting room floor in front of the fire when he came in after his tea. It was late and the other children had already been put to bed. She had been allowed to stay up. She had a Big Job to do. She had to make sure that there was a glass of milk and a piece of Christmas cake left on the sideboard for Santa. And she couldn't forget Rudolph! An extra-large carrot would help him to pull the heavy sleigh.

'What are you doing in here all on your own?' Daddy asked, in his strange, tired voice.

He sat into the armchair, and she went over to sit in his lap.

'I was just thinking about Santa and hoping the fire wouldn't hurt him when he comes down the chimney tonight,' she whispered.

The funny, tired voice said: 'You know you're my best girl?'

'I do, Daddy,' she answered.

'And you know I think you're a very smart girl?'

'I do, Daddy.'

'Well then, tell me this,' he said. 'How could a great big girl of eight years old believe... ?'

And he whispered the secret of generations.

She looked at him, aghast.

'It's not true, Daddy,' she cried. 'It can't be true!'

The biggest lump imaginable formed in the little girl's throat. Her eyes welled up. She couldn't look at Daddy or stay in the room any longer. Racing upstairs to her bedroom, she buried her head under the pillow. She sobbed until she thought her heart would break.

Later, Mum came to tuck her in and to say her prayers. The child's red, swollen face told its own tale.

'What on earth happened?' Mum asked, frightened to see the child so distressed.

Between snuffles and sobs and hiccups, the story came out.

Mum remained quiet for a minute.

She stroked the little girl's forehead and with a tissue, helped to wipe the tears from her eyes.

'You know,' she said, 'when your father was a little boy...'

'Daddy was a little boy?' the little girl asked.

'Oh yes,' said Mum with a smile. 'When your Daddy was a little boy, he had nobody to love him. He was sent away from his own Mammy and Daddy because times were hard. Things were different back then.'

The little girl didn't really understand, but she nodded, and sobbed a little less.

'So, your Daddy made a promise that he would always love his own children and do his very best for them.'

The little girl frowned.

'The reason he said what he said tonight,' Mum continued, 'is that he was afraid you loved Santa more than you loved him. He was just a bit jealous of Santa Claus.'

The little girl's mind was churning.

'Now close your eyes and go to sleep,' Mum whispered. 'And, in the morning, don't say anything about this to your brothers and sisters.'

Mum kissed the little girl, tucked the blanket around her, and said: 'Goodnight, my little angel!'

Raised voices could be heard from downstairs as the child fell into an exhausted slumber.

Christmas never had quite the same magic again.

The Dead Language Teacher

I slipped into a pew at the back of the cathedral. The familiar soaring ceilings, stained-glass windows, walls adorned with beautiful frescoes and sculptures, and floors of polished marble brought me back to my childhood days growing up nearby. A small girl picking blackberries along the ruined walls of the Old Gaol. From the window of our house on Canal Road, we saw the new building gradually rising like a phoenix.

As a child I came here with my family to twelve o'clock mass every Sunday. I especially loved when my brother sang the treble solo from the choir balcony. Even though I became agnostic in my teens, and my heart is firmly set against the institutions of the Catholic Church, this building has never failed to make me feel calm and soothed.

In front of me, a congregation of mourners filled the pews. Candles flickered warmly beside the coffin in front of the altar. A faint scent of candle wax filled the air, intermingled with a hint of incense, and flowers from a previous ceremony. The organ played sombre music, interrupted intermittently by a murmur of conversation or an occasional sob.

Waiting for the ceremony to start, my mind began to drift. Fifth Year. The school a hotbed of adolescent energy. Our group of girls, full of mischief and rebellion, giggling and whispering -

the latest gossip, the hottest boys. How often did we sneak out of the school grounds for a clandestine rendezvous, nascent hormones raging through our bloodstreams? *'Let's go for a smoke. Or a quick snog?'* Boys from the nearby secondary school and students from the university were on hand to supply both. Studying was the last thing on our minds.

It was a badge of honour to be a rebel. The corridors echoed with laughter at our latest circumvention of the rules. Our pranks were legendary. The Hulk Convention was a classic. We dyed the fountain green and immersed ourselves, uniforms and all, to emerge as strange creatures from outer space. It took ages to remove the dye from our skin. The uniforms never recovered. Someone thought of renaming the hit song to *A Whiter Shade of Green.*

When we convinced the school principal to allow us to have a 'girls only' dance in the gym, inevitably it was infiltrated by boys who discovered easy access through open windows and unlocked doors. How were we to know that the opposite sex would arrive? Many of them wore wigs and dresses. I'm sure our parents secretly smiled at these antics when they were summoned for the principal's disciplinary meeting. Innocent enough times. Always looking for new ways to have fun, creativity knowing no bounds.

The first day I met Miss Maguire, I sensed that things were about to change. She was a tall, formidable woman with a strong, sturdy frame that looked as though it could take on the world. Her voice, though, was surprisingly gentle and soothing, like a warm cup of tea on a cold winter's day. Maybe she hoped to get our attention by striding purposefully into the noisy Latin Room and scrawling her name in large, uneven letters on the blackboard. But ignoring her efforts, thirty girls continued to laugh and talk all at once, their voices echoing off the walls – walls that were decorated with maps of the Roman Empire and Latin phrases. *Fac silentium!* was positioned prominently above the blackboard.

'Quiet, please!'

The noise did not decrease by a decibel.

'Fac silentium!' Miss Maguire tried again. This time she scraped her fingernails along the blackboard, and the effect was immediate. The chatting and giggling gave way to a hushed silence and an idle curiosity. *Who was this creature with fingernails like prongs? Was that an odour of chalk dust? or a faint scent of perfume?*

As we filed back to our desks and settled in, I couldn't help but notice the slight tremble in Miss Maguire's hands as she surveyed the sea of expectant faces before her. Her tweed jacket, with its unmistakable sleeves, peeked out from beneath her black academic gown, and her hair, an unremarkable shade of brown, appeared to have been chopped haphazardly with a blunt knife. Perched halfway down her nose, a pair of square-rimmed glasses added to her studious demeanour.

With a sense of purpose, Miss Maguire retrieved her worn leather satchel from the desk beside her. As she rummaged inside, we could see the corners of textbooks and papers peeking out. With a flourish, she laid out her materials on the desk before us, each book and paper placed with meticulous care.

'This book,' she said, holding up a green-covered volume, 'is *Kennedy's Latin Primer*. It will become your bible for the next two years.'

There was a hushed silence in the classroom, broken only by the shuffling of feet and the occasional whisper. We exchanged glances, and a few of us couldn't help but snigger. Miss Maguire's cheeks flushed as she searched for the culprit. 'You!' she exclaimed, pointing directly at me. 'To the blackboard.' My heart racing, I stumbled from my desk and approached the top of the class.

'Take this chalk and write the following: *Salve. Tibi omnes obviam delector.*'

I struggled to get the words down, my guesses proving less than hopeless. I had to ask the teacher to spell the words for me, and even then, it took me a long time to write them correctly.

'What's your name, girl?' Miss Maguire asked when I had finished.

'Sophia, Miss,' I mumbled, my face burning with embarrassment.

'The Latin name *Sophia* means "wisdom". You must live up to your name. Now back to your seat, Sophia.'

Face ablaze, I returned to my seat.

'Girls, get your dictionaries out. Make sense of the words on the board.'

Oblivious to our stunned faces, she continued as if nothing had happened. 'Latin is not all about grammar, you know? There are hugely interesting stories in Roman History. Hands up who has heard about Anthony and Cleopatra?' All hands in the classroom shot up.

'See,' she said triumphantly. 'You have made inroads into Roman history already. Now girls, for the next two years we will concern ourselves with the study of the Latin language, the reading of some Classical Latin authors, and learning about Roman History, Art, and Literature.' She paused, looking intently at us.

'Any questions?'

We shuffled in our seats, too embarrassed to speak.

'It mightn't seem like the most exciting topic in the world,' she continued, 'but I promise if you pay attention and work hard, a world will open up for you that will change your lives forever. Latin can teach you so much. It will lay deep foundations for any language you speak or plan to learn.'

Miss Maguire shook her head pensively. 'Of course, only the few will benefit. Many will fall by the wayside. The clever ones, the girls who wish to make something of themselves, those are the girls that will excel not only in the study of Latin, but in acquiring a wealth of knowledge for other languages as well. *Mihi crede, hoc fiet!*'

She was speaking gibberish as far as we were concerned.

'Now,' she said, 'did anyone solve the sentence on the blackboard?'

There was a clamour in the cloakroom after the class, as we tried to outdo each other with our mean comments.

'Ugh, did you see what she was wearing? So outdated!' said Siobhan, rolling her eyes.

'Was she even wearing a bra?' chimed in Aoife, causing the others to giggle.

'Looks like a throwback from the fifties!' I joined in, shaking my head in disapproval.

'So boring!' complained Marion, crossing her arms. 'I can't believe *she's* teaching us Latin!'

'And scraping her nails like that!' added Niamh. 'My ears are still splitting!'

'Spouting Latin phrases. As if anyone would want to speak that 'dead' language. I could barely stay awake in the class. She's so dull!' said Siobhan, again.

'And such a bog accent!' said Aoife, mimicking their teacher's voice.

'Imagine being so old! I mean, she must be at least in her fifties!' said Jen, making a face.

'Look! I made a drawing of her sitting with her legs wide apart!' said Marion, holding up her notebook and causing the group to burst into laughter.

'When she picked on me to write on the blackboard, I nearly died! I didn't even know what she was saying, never mind trying to spell the words,' I chimed in.

The girls started chanting, taunting me with silly insults. 'Sophia, Wisdom, Brainy Box! Teacher's pet!' '

I wanted them to know I was just as tough and cool as they were.

'Shut up, losers! You're just jealous!' I scoffed, as I stuffed my Latin copybook underneath the rest of my books. On the first page I had written:

Salve. Tibi omnes obviam delector = 'Hello, you all I am pleased to meet?'

It wasn't long until Miss Maguire had our measure. Her frustration with our lack of interest in Latin began to show. 'Giddy goats!' she would exclaim, Ninnies! Airheads!' We couldn't help but giggle at her expressions, although they were a bit hurtful.

We decided that a prank was called for.

The Brains Trust, my four friends Marion, Siobhan, Aisling, Niamh, and I, had come up with the perfect plan for Operation Hot Air. We tumbled into the newly opened party shop in the city, drawn in by the colourful balloons on display. 'Look at these,' Aisling exclaimed, grabbing a balloon with a cartoon girl's face on it. 'These are perfect!'

We laughed out loud as we cycled home from town, balloons bouncing behind us. Our plan was to replace ourselves with these silly balloons, so that when Miss Maguire opened the door, she would be greeted with desks occupied by real 'Airheads.'

The excitement was palpable as we sneaked into school before anyone else arrived. The five of us moved like a well-oiled machine, each with our designated task to complete. We blew the balloons up and experimented with the helium to achieve perfect high-pitched squeaky voices. We were careful not to burst any balloons, holding back our laughter as we worked towards our goal.

We approached the Latin Room, our hearts beating with anticipation. Skulking around the corridors, we moved like commandos on a secret mission. We were all sweating, and our uniforms were sticking to our skin. We burst into the room, closed the door, and quickly got to work. We each tied balloons to our desks and chortled with delight as we surveyed our handiwork. Suddenly, the door handle began to turn. We froze. Panic swept through the room like a tidal wave. We were doomed. We would be caught for sure. And then, just as quickly as it had started, the door handle stopped turning. Our hearts were pounding in our chests. We huddled together, trying to control our breathing and not make a sound. And then, finally, after what felt like an eternity, the sound of the caretaker's footsteps faded away.

We waited a few more minutes just to be sure, and then we cautiously emerged from our hiding places. We had narrowly escaped.

'Yesss!' Siobhan exclaimed, high on helium and excitement. 'We did it! Now let's get out of here!'

But I had one more thing to do. I marched up to the blackboard, the scene of my earlier humiliation, picked up the chalk, and wrote in big letters:

LATIN IS A LANGUAGE
AS DEAD AS DEAD CAN BE
IT KILLED THE ANCIENT ROMANS
AND NOW IT'S KILLING ME.

'Now we can go!' I said happily.

As soon as were off the school grounds, we fell about laughing. The joy of having successfully executed our prank, and now having the complete day to ourselves, was overwhelming. We headed for the beach.

'That was gas!' exclaimed Aisling, pride shining in her eyes.

'Gas, all right!' I said.

Marion, ever the cautious one, added, 'But we need to be careful. If anyone sees us, we're really in for it!

Siobhan, rummaging through her backpack, produced a packet of cigarettes. 'Anyone want one?' she asked with a mischievous grin.

Niamh hesitated, 'I don't know, what if someone sees us smoking in public wearing our uniforms? We'd really be done for then!

'Oh, come on, Niamh,' Siobhan cajoled, 'we're not hurting anyone. It'll be fun.'

Tittering nervously, we took turns, puffing and coughing simultaneously. We felt so grown-up, and we savoured the delicious tension between enjoying ourselves and breaking the rules in such a rebellious way.

We were laughing and smoking when a group of boys from the neighbouring school appeared. One of them, a tall, dark-haired boy, sauntered over.

'Hey, mind if we join you?'

Before long, Sean was passing around a bottle of cider. We all took a swig, trying to act like the burning sensation in our throats was the most natural thing in the world.

As the day ended, reality with a sense of sadness and anxiety overtook us. What if our parents found out? Would we be expelled from school?

'It was worth it, right?' said Siobhan, breaking the silence.

The next morning, as we stood before the stern school principal, our hearts were heavy with dread. Sister Aloysius, dressed in her full habit, glared at us with disapproval.

'I cannot understand, with all respect, why you girls would treat a new teacher in this school in such a manner, playing your silly pranks,' she admonished us. 'Not to mention absconding, smoking in public in your school uniforms and drinking with boys at the beach.'

We looked at each other furtively. How did she know everything? How did she find out?

'You will stay back for detention today and for the rest of this month. And I intend to telephone your parents and inform them of exactly what you got up to yesterday. Your telephone numbers please.'

Our heads hung low as each girl gave her home number to the principal. When it was my turn, I felt a knot form in my stomach.

'Sister, our phone number is ex-directory, and I'm not allowed to give it to anyone without permission,' I said.

The nun's eyes narrowed as she glowered at me. 'Ask for permission when you go home for lunch and come and see me immediately afterwards with your telephone number,' she ordered.

After lunch, I tried to sneak in the side door to avoid the principal's gaze, but she caught me.

'Well, girl, what is your telephone number?' she demanded.

I clapped my hand to my mouth in feigned remorse. 'Oh, I forgot, Sister. I forgot to ask for permission.'

Sister Aloysius let out an exasperated sigh. 'Do not test my patience, young lady. Go home and ask your parents for permission. And make sure to bring me your telephone number first thing tomorrow morning.'

As I walked away, I knew that I had only delayed the inevitable. My parents would find out before too long. My father would be furious at me for bunking out of Latin, of all subjects. 'Why couldn't you dodge something irrelevant, like home economics?' I could imagine him raving.

Back in the Latin Room, Miss Maguire looked at us with a mixture of disbelief and disappointment.

'I expected better from you girls,' she said, shaking her head. 'This is a place of learning, not a circus.'

We felt chastened, but we also knew that we would never forget the thrill of the previous day, the sense of adventure and camaraderie that had brought us together. And we knew that, despite our carry-on, Miss Maguire would never forget us either.

The merciless criticism, backbiting and caricaturing of poor Miss Maguire continued until we found someone new to taunt – the first male teacher in the school, I think. By then Miss Maguire had become old news, and a new target for our energies was found.

As time wore on, I began to see Miss Maguire as a fine teacher, and grudgingly admitted that she was doing an excellent job.

It was not until my brother brought home his Roman History book from boarding school, and I saw that the author of the textbook was Miss Maguire, that I realised just how accomplished she really was. How could I have doubted her expertise in the subject?

Under her patient tuition, my Latin improved exponentially, and I knew I had her to thank for my excellent grade in the Leaving Certificate.

In the last conversation I ever had with her, she gave me advice that stayed with me for the rest of my life. She told me to pursue Latin at university, convinced that this was where my talents lay.

I didn't bring a gift to thank her for all her efforts; we didn't do that in the seventies. But I hoped she knew how much impact she had on my life.

I was brought back from my reverie as the priest began the funeral service. The mourners joined in the prayers, their voices a soothing hum that filled the cathedral with a sense of calm. The readings were delivered with reverence. The hymns were nostalgic and dated. I joined in quietly, singing *Faith of Our Fathers* and *Lady of Knock*.

As the service ended. Miss Maguire's nephew, Noel, took the podium to deliver the eulogy. He spoke about his aunt Catherine's life – 'Catty, we called her' - her devotion to the church, her love of Latin, and her dedication to her family. I felt the weight of my past actions bearing down on me. The memory of how we had treated Miss Maguire flooded my mind – the cruel jokes, the relentless teasing, the backbiting. As her life story unfolded, my face reddened with shame and remorse. I didn't know she was once a nun. I never considered the emotions she must have felt when she left the religious life. She had left a headmistress's role to join our school as a new teacher in a lowly position. How demeaning that must have been. It never occurred to me that she had a family who loved her. Noel highlighted her many gifts. He spoke of her kindness, her generosity, and her abundant talents. I realised that I had never appreciated her as a person or recognised her as being a remarkable individual. I never even knew her first name.

The coffin was carried out of the church. I followed behind, my head bowed in respect. I whispered to Miss Maguire as I walked, 'I'm sorry, so sorry...' It was a small gesture, but it felt like the right thing to do.

Stepping out of the church into the bright sunlight, I heard a voice calling my name.

'Sophia! Wait!'

It was Noel, the nephew. I turned to face him, surprised by his sudden approach.

'Thank you for coming,' he said. 'Sorry for startling you. I know your face from my aunt's scrapbooks.'

'Her scrapbooks?'

'Yes, she followed the careers of all her students, but she had a soft spot for your class.'

My eyebrows shot up in surprise. 'Is that so? I had no idea.'

'Oh, yes. She really enjoyed your antics. She especially remembered your balloon prank. She had a tough time keeping a straight face when she had to tell you off about it next day. But she was such a professional, she never let on how much she enjoyed it.'

He smiled. 'Do you know, she even brought the balloons home to my sister and me and showed us how to do squeaky voices! We'd never seen helium balloons before!'

Noel looked over at the hearse and the crowd milling around it.

'She always said there was more to the Prankster Class than just pranks. You worked hard and you succeeded. Seventeen of you went to university, and five of you even did Latin for your degrees. Catty was so proud of you when you got your doctorate.'

I was flabbergasted. I wanted to run away as far as possible. I needed a place to cry in private.

'I'm so sorry,' I mumbled. 'I've an urgent appointment...'

'Yes, yes, of course,' he said offering me his hand. 'Look at you now, Dr Timms, a busy university professor. Aunt Catherine's legacy lives on.'

I ran to my car and drove away, feeling grateful for the lessons she had taught me, even if they were learned too late.

Rural Life

Getting on with Act Three

We pulled up at the beach in our battered old Toyota Starlet. 15th November – three years to the day since that life-changing ceremony on Barna Pier, and the 'party to end all parties' in the Twelve. It was the opening scene of our second act. Nearing retirement now, we had spent most of our lives struggling to be accepted in our own country. At last, we could be ourselves, openly, without fear or scorn. The 'just married' sign still stood boldly on the car's parcel shelf. We left it there, along with a smattering of confetti, as a reminder to ourselves and to everyone else that we lived in a new Ireland.

When we first met in Dublin in the 1980s – my God, life was so different. Ours was the traditional 'love that dared not speak its name'. Spending Saturday afternoons at the Bailey pub in Duke Street was like belonging to a secret society. For many years, our families did not know. We 'made do' with furtive holidays abroad and snatched weekends in European cities.

There was nothing good about being gay in Ireland in the 1980s. From about 1983 or 1984, people in the gay community started to get sick. Some developed terrible facial growths, others experienced massive weight loss, or coughs that just would not go away. And one day, they were gone. Disappeared. Later, you'd hear they had died.

When we moved to Galway, life got a bit easier. We both worked in the university. We were part of an accepting community. The 2015 campaign was amazing! We lived most of our adult lives not caring about marriage – it was a straight gig, with religious overtones, and it wasn't our thing. But when everything changed, we realised we actually wanted a wedding – not a civil ceremony or any other substitute, but the real thing – confetti, rings, cake and, of course, a marriage certificate.

Naturally, we were made uncomfortable by the views of some conservative religious types around the place who really hated the gays. It was an opportunity for all the nasty bigots to have their say. Our local priest made a name for himself with his forceful arguments against same-sex marriage. But, on the day we married, we smiled as we realised – they can rant all they want now, it's over, it's done. Time for us to get on with our lives.

Then it happened. Tom got sick. Something had lain dormant for all those years but now I was recognising the all too familiar symptoms, and so was he. On this particular evening, the 'just married' sign still rattling around in the back of the car, we drove to the beach to remember the beautiful November sunset when we made our wedding vows.

We pulled in to our customary spot. To our left we had a full view back into Galway City along the bay. But to the right, a shiny BMW car was parked in such a way that it completely occluded the view of the pier where our ceremony was held.

Churning up inside, and fuming at the unfairness of it all, I got out of the car and hailed a passer-by, an elderly man with a black Labrador.

'Who owns that car, d'you know?' I demanded. 'It couldn't be parked in a worse place. Tom here hasn't long to live, and he finds great peace looking out at the bay. Could we get the owner to move it, do you think?'

'I doubt it. That's Father Simony's car,' said the man. 'He's down there on the beach having his evening swim.'

Sure enough, when I looked out towards the sea, I could see a naked figure on the rocks, towelling his hair, at ease with the world.

'Bastard!' I shouted. 'Bigoted bastard!' And with that I started to kick the front tyres of the BMW.

Always willing to support me in whatever I did, poor Tom got out and started kicking too.

'Come on, lads!' said the man with the black Labrador. 'That's not the answer!'

The priest heard the commotion and, quite forgetting about his towel, started to run towards us.

We landed a few more kicks on the shiny surface of the car. The bodywork had a number of dents and scrapes after our efforts. The naked priest was leaping over the rocks, getting closer and closer.

'We'd better hightail it!' I said to Tom and we both leapt back into the car. I revved up the Toyota and sped away in a cloud of exhaust fumes and gravel. In the rear-view mirror, I could see Fr Simony in his pelt, waving his fist in anger at our disappearing vehicle.

'Let the man with the Labrador explain,' I said to Tom. 'We've argued long enough. Let's just get on with Act Three.'

The Redbridge Show

Bea was lovingly polishing the Perpetual Trophy when she heard the soft plop of a letter landing on the doormat. How she loved the trophy! When she handled it, she could almost hear the applause and she relived the moment when her embroidered tablecloth was crowned as the county show's premier needlework exhibit for the third year running.

She dropped the duster and went to pick up the letter that changed everything.

The little family lived in a small town in Mayo. Kitty and Bea were sisters, and Seán was Kitty's husband. He was a tall, bulky Garda Sergeant, who took up a lot of space, so much so that the rest of the world had to work around him. No-one knew if he spoke much down at the barracks, but he never opened his mouth at home.

There was no need, as the diminutive women, Kitty especially, were great talkers – indeed, years later, it was said of Kitty that she died in mid-sentence.

Their house was a sensible, grey, 1920s structure built onto the road with only a narrow footpath separating it from the traffic. A shiny, canary-yellow door lifted the greyness of the building, and the burnished brass knocker glinted in the occasional sunshine.

Inside, the house was small and pokey. The hall door opened into a corridor, leading straight to the back door – an odd arrangement, put in place by the previous owner to lead his horse through to the back yard. To the right of this corridor, there was a small downstairs area and a steep stairs leading up to the bedrooms. The tiny sitting room was bursting with photos, ornaments and other memorabilia; the windows framed by báinin curtains with hand embroidered Celtic symbols snaking up their length. There was barely room to sit by the ever-blazing open fire. When there was a crowd in, damp handkerchiefs mopping sweaty brows were much in evidence.

Behind the house rose a majestic back garden, culminating in a beautiful orchard on the hilltop. Opposite the front door, and across the road, was the entrance to their other garden. Sloping down to the salmon-laden river, it was cultivated with an abundance of vegetables and fruit bushes.

They were industrious people. Kitty was a primary teacher in the Brothers, and Bea was the postmistress, like her mother before her. The sisters had moved with their mother from Dublin to their county of origin when their father died from TB in the 1930s. Both parents worked for the Department of Posts & Telegraphs, and, unlike the thousands of people who claimed to be there, they really did witness the 1916 Rising when it began inside the GPO.

The trio worked hard all day in their jobs as minor public servants, but their creativity blossomed in the long evenings. Kitty used her magical wizardry to bake mouth-watering cakes and buns, sugary, delicate and delicious confections that everyone loved – and loved Kitty for. Bea was a gifted needlewoman. Using patterns – or her imagination – she could do

The Redbridge Show

anything with those hands of hers. Between knitting for the missions, crocheting, smocking, and crafting hand-made toys, she was a cottage industry in her own right, with an abundance of patience and an evident inner tranquillity.

The family benefited from delicious meals, enjoying home-grown marrows, potatoes, rhubarb, beetroot, carrots, cabbage, onions, and, in summer, the peas, radishes, runner beans and courgettes that Seán grew in the sloping, riverside garden. Everyone helped to cultivate the orchard and they grew a few delphiniums as well, but not too many flowers as they were more concerned with putting food on the table. A self-sufficient unit, they made their own clothes, grew their own vegetables and frequently feasted on salmon from the river below. There wasn't much time to socialise or make friends.

Every August, there was a big county show in Redbridge. The large indoor section featured cookery, vegetables, plants, handicrafts and more, pitting neighbour against neighbour in spirited competition.

One year, Kitty, Bea and Seán resolved to make their mark and submit their baking, needlework and vegetables to the show for exhibition and judging. Unspoken amongst them was the thought that this might help them to integrate better into the community and perhaps strike up some friendships with like-minded locals.

Initially, they won some of the lesser prizes, but, undeterred, they redoubled their efforts and strove for even better results as the years went by. They started to enjoy themselves and relished the competitive edge that had crept into their lives.

In their first really good year, Bea was crowned the overall winner in the Handicrafts category, with special mention for her embroidered tablecloth; Kitty waltzed away with first prize for her Victoria Sponge. Seán came first with his splendid display of vegetables as well as securing the trophy for Biggest Marrow. After that, they were a 'shoe-in', as the locals used to say. The Redbridge Show became the highlight of their year, and the dull days at the end of August were animated with talk of bigger and better plans for next year.

Rain hail or shine, Bea trudged up to the Post Office. She opened up diligently and was never late. Her day was given over to dealing with the customers. She listened patiently to their small complaints and gossip. She went home for lunch, returning to despatch the four o'clock post and finishing her day off as calmly and capably as she had begun it.

Everything was going so well until the letter came. Still clutching the precious Perpetual Trophy, Bea picked up the envelope from the doormat and examined it, before opening it up and reading the scrawl on a page torn from a child's school copybook.

'Why don't ye blow-ins get out of the Redbridge Show and give the local people a chance to win.'

The note was not signed.

With a weight on her heart, Bea went back to work in the afternoon and thought about what she might do. A couple of days later, armed with the Perpetual Trophy, she went to see Mr

Lenihan, who ran the show for the locality. She told him how she had received an anonymous letter, suggesting that the family stop entering for the Redbridge Show, and that it was her intention not to put in any entries this year. Kitty and Seán, she said, would not be entering either. And he could have his trophy back.

Mr Lenihan blanched, and beads of perspiration emerged on his bald pate.

'But, Bea,' he cried, 'this is terrible! This goes against the whole spirit of the Redbridge Show. You must reconsider. Of course, you must continue to enter the show.'

The response came in the form of Bea's stubborn shake of the head, the setting of her lips and her firm statement: 'No, you won't see any more entries from my family in the Redbridge Show.'

Mr Lenihan scratched his head again and, when he spoke, there was disappointment in his voice. 'Bea, the three of you are the stars of the show. It wouldn't be the same without you. Will you not ignore this nonsense and reconsider?'

A stamp of the foot, a shake of the head and another firm 'No'.

Mr Lenihan could barely speak.

'Bea,' he faltered. 'Do you have any idea who might have written this to you?'

'Do I have any idea? Of course I have. Don't forget I've been in the Post Office in Redbridge for 25 years. There isn't a hand in this village that I don't recognise.'

And she turned on her heel, an indignant little robin, leaving Mr Lenihan in some distress.

For them, that was the end of the Redbridge Show. Of course, Bea didn't tell anyone who had written the letter, apart from Kitty and Seán. It was noticed that life got a bit harder for Joe Flynn from the village. He seemed to be always picking up poaching fines these days, and he had to stop taking his car to the pub. And then, there was the inquiry that brought to light that Mrs Flynn, who won the knitting competition by submitting the same geansaí every year, was not even the actual manufacturer of the garment. The item of clothing was, in fact, made by her cousin in Castlebar.

What's definite is that interest in the show seemed to decline after that, with fewer and fewer entries in the competitions, until it finally petered out altogether. And, in her later years, Bea let slip that Mrs Flynn had come into the Post Office one day and burst out: 'Why did ye pull out of the show like that? Ye ruined it for everyone else.'

Faraway Hills

It was a typical October Tuesday night on the island, with the tourists gone for the season and the winds picking up their pace. Rain poured down in sheets, drenching the landscape outside. Mam rose from the tea table and started clearing the dishes, while Dad reclined in his chair and lit another cigarette. The radio news concluded, replaced by a lively pop song blaring through the speakers – England's victorious entry for Eurovision, *Puppet on a String.*

'Ironic, isn't it?' thought Máire grimly, joining her mother at the sink to help with the stack of dishes on the draining board. She gazed out at the rain pelting the windowpane, drying the crockery and cutlery as she contemplated her predicament.

'What in the world am I doing here? I'm trapped for good on this desolate rock in the middle of the Atlantic. At least when Micheál and Pádraic were around, there was some fun to be had. Mam is so melancholy, Dad is perpetually irritable, and I've got no escape,' she lamented silently.

Dad began fiddling with the radio, much to Mam's curiosity. 'What are you up to?' she inquired.

'I can't bear listening to that rubbish! I'm switching over to the BBC,' he declared.

As expected, the theme tune of *The Archers* soon filled the air, and her parents settled down to enjoy their beloved radio soap. Máire, taking advantage of the diversion, slipped quietly out of the kitchen and made her way up to her room.

From underneath her bed, she retrieved a cardboard suitcase and inspected its contents. A few articles of clothing, a pair of high boots, magazines – *Jackie* and *New Musical Express*, and a package of letters from her cousin Eibhlín, tied together with a ribbon. These items – her secret treasures – held immense value for her. Without cousin Eibhlín, Máire would be lost. Okay, she could listen to Radio Luxembourg at night and occasionally get her hands on a magazine with the latest news, gossip, and interviews featuring the likes of the Beatles, the Stones, the Searchers, Cilla, Dusty, and the rest. But Eibhlín, she was truly living!

Máire perused the letters repeatedly, devouring every detail that Eibhlín so thoughtfully shared. It had been a year since Eibhlín had emigrated to England. Working for various secretarial agencies, she was sent to different offices all over London. One week she could be stationed in Bond Street, the next in Brentwood.

She lived in a shared flat near Baker Street, close enough to walk to Oxford Street for late-night shopping. Eibhlín fancied herself 'a dedicated follower of fashion.' Mini-skirts, hot pants, boots, ankle-length coats – she owned them all. Her Saturdays were spent exploring the trendy King's Road. The fashion choices of the girls there would surely give Mam and Dad a heart attack. Eibhlín shopped for mod clothes in Carnaby Street, Harrods' Way In, Biba, and Portobello Road street market. Although Máire had never been to London, she felt intimately acquainted with the city through Eibhlín's vivid letters.

In the evenings, Eibhlín and her friends would frequent clubs or attend lively gatherings. One of her friends even had a boyfriend who knew Oliver Reed, and Eibhlín had once attended a party at his house. She sported peace symbols like everyone else, though her interests didn't extend to politics. However, she did walk past Grosvenor Square during the massive anti-Vietnam demonstration led by Tariq Ali outside the US Embassy.

Lost in her treasures, Máire carefully selected a tie-dyed t-shirt and bell-bottom jeans. The jeans were adorned with flower patches and peace symbols. She added a sheepskin vest that looked stylish over the t-shirt, and topped it all off with a sailor's cap, just like Twiggy. Finally, she threw on her old school coat to conceal her outfit and headed downstairs.

She poked her head into the kitchen where Mam and Dad were, and nervously announced, 'Mam and Dad, I'm going over to the pub to see Eibhlín. She's back from London for a few days.'

Mam looked up from her knitting and expressed concern. 'Máire, my love, what are you doing going out on a night like this? Why don't you stay here with us where it's warm? We can have a cup of tea and listen to the news together.'

Máire's heartstrings tugged at her, but this time she mustered the courage to assert herself. 'Mam, I really want to see Eibhlín. It's been a whole year since she's been home, and she has so much news. I'm dying to hear all about it.'

Máire hung her wet coat in the porch and entered the crowded and boisterous pub. Amongst the familiar faces, there was no mistaking Eibhlín. Surrounded by local lads, she stood out, in her black and white geometric print dress. Máire could tell it was a miniskirt, barely covering the essentials. She had three drinks lined up in front of her. Máire knew from the letters that Eibhlín's favourite tipple was Bloody Mary.

Máire's eyes scanned the room, taking in the lively scene. One person caught her attention - a young man sitting beside Eibhlín whom she didn't recognise. With a hint of shyness, Máire sidled up to her cousin, and they embraced tightly for a long moment. Eibhlín paused their hug to introduce her companion.

'Peter, this is Máire, my cousin. I've told you all about her. Peter is one of my London cousins, Máire. We travelled over together.'

Caught off guard, Máire looked directly into the stranger's eyes. He had a mischievous look, reminiscent of Davy Jones, her heartthrob from The Monkees, with his shiny dark hair that flowed down the back.

She managed to utter, 'Tá fáilte romhat,' and Peter winked in response, saying, 'Nice to meet ya!' in what Máire suspected was a London accent.

The two girls delved into animated conversation. Máire couldn't help but notice Peter's growing interest in her. When Eibhlín turned to greet another person, Peter leaned closer to Máire.

'Can I buy you a drink, love?' he asked, surprising her.

She replied, taken aback, 'No, just a glass of water, please.'

Peter swiftly returned from the bar with a pint of Guinness and a glass of water. He sat down beside her, and they continued to chat. Peter shared that he worked on a Ford assembly line in Dagenham, where he was well paid but bored.

Taking a sip of his pint, he asked, 'So, what about you? Are you still in school?'

Máire shook her head. 'No, I finished secondary school on the mainland last year. I really wanted to go to university, but that wasn't on the cards.'

Furrowing his brow inquisitively, Peter pressed further, 'Why not? What happened?'

Máire let out a sigh and replied, 'Ah, you wouldn't understand. I'm needed here at home.'

Curiosity filled Peter's eyes as he asked, 'But don't you have any brothers or sisters who can take care of things?'

'I have two older brothers,' Máire answered, her voice tinged with a touch of sadness. 'But now it's just me, Mam, and Dad.'

Peter nodded, trying to grasp the situation. 'Oh, so they must be elderly, then? They can't manage on their own?'

Máire quickly clarified, 'No, they can manage just fine. Dad still goes fishing, and Mam keeps busy with the B&B during the summer. In the winter, she enjoys a bit of a rest, sitting down, listening to *The Archers,* and knitting.'

Peter asked, 'If they're doing well, then why are you needed here?'

Máire hesitated for a moment, her voice trembling slightly. 'It's just... they're lonely. They don't have anyone else here.'

Concern flickered in Peter's eyes as he probed further, 'And where are your brothers?'

'Micheál is in America,' Máire answered, a hint of worry in her voice. 'We're all so concerned about him. He joined the army, and now there's a possibility he'll be sent to Vietnam.'

'You said you have two brothers. What about the other one?' Peter gently inquired.

'Pádraic,' Máire murmured, her eyes welling up with tears. 'Pádraic couldn't bear the weight of island life anymore. We knew he was unhappy, but we only truly understood the depth of it when we found his broken body at the bottom of the cliff.'

A heavy silence hung in the air as Máire gathered herself before continuing, 'So, you see, I'm stuck here. This isn't what I want. All I want is to live, laugh, and have some adventure. But it's never going to happen here.'

Peter reached for his pint but hesitated, unsure of what to say next. As he searched for the right words, he glanced around the pub, noticing the modern features like the jukebox and pool table that Tí Flatharta boasted.

'Would you like to play pool?' he finally offered, hoping to divert their conversation to something lighter.

Máire mustered a small smile and shook her head. 'No thanks.'

'Okay, then,' Peter suggested, a glimmer of inspiration crossing his face. 'What about I play a song for you on the jukebox?'

With a quick stride, he returned from the jukebox, excitement shining in his eyes. 'This one is new. Bet you haven't heard it before.'

A sudden hush fell over the pub as the sweet melody of a small string orchestra filled the room, followed by Paul McCartney's familiar voice. *Wednesday morning, at five o'clock, as the day begins...*

Máire found herself entranced, her heart pounding as she absorbed every word of the poignant ballad. When the song ended, she turned to Peter, her voice filled with determination.

'Did you hear that? Every word... Paul could be talking about me! That girl he sings about, it could be me! It's a sign! I've made up my mind! I'm going!'

Overwhelmed with emotions, she pulled a piece of paper from her handbag, fighting back tears as she began to write:

'*Dear Mam and Dad...*'

Working World

Evie's First Job

'You're very welcome to Andrew Quill Solicitors,' declared the prim and stern-looking woman who greeted her at the threshold. 'I am Miss Whisker, the supervisor of the typing pool,' she introduced herself, with an air of importance that permeated the cold morning air.

Evie drew her coat closer against the biting September breeze, mentally bracing herself for what was to come. Having left the embrace of County Galway behind, this was her first job since graduating from secretarial college at the beginning of the summer. Oh, how she had enjoyed the freedom of the past few months! Mornings that seemed to glow brighter with each passing day, afternoons spent helping her mother in their sunlit kitchen filled with the fragrance of home-cooked meals, and evenings consumed with gleeful frolics with her brothers amid the serenity of their farm. But that life felt like a cherished memory now that she stood on the precipice of a new chapter.

'Let's not dally,' Miss Whisker broke through her reverie, 'I'll show you your workspace and detail your responsibilities. You'll find we are not as daunting as we might seem at first. Follow me.' With these words, she swiftly turned towards the grand staircase that branched off the reception hall, her heels echoing a staccato rhythm on the polished marble floor.

Evie's eyes had been drawn to the staircase during her interview – it spiralled like an elegant spine of the building into an abyss of anticipation. The ceilings soared above her, their height enough to demand three ladders stacked on top of one another. The magnificence of her surroundings, particularly the intricate plasterwork adorning the covings, had left her in silent awe during her first visit. It was so different from the cloistered back room where her interview was held, a space that seemed to languish in a perpetual gloom.

Guided by the silken touch of the mahogany banister, Evie ascended the stairs, following Miss Whisker's stern silhouette. At the top, the lady paused, then sharply turned right to knock on a majestic hardwood door. Receiving no answer, she gestured Evie into a room that radiated sunlight through the vast windows overlooking St Stephen's Green. The world outside was abuzz with traffic, the ceaseless hum of city life contrasting with the serene sight of iron railings sheltering trees ablaze with autumnal hues. Students, just like her not long ago, wandered and laughed amongst the foliage. A pang of nostalgia struck Evie, the scene evoking a bittersweet sense of the past.

A tart voice brought her back to reality. Straightening her back, she refocused on Miss Whisker's instructions. 'Mr Quill usually graces us with his presence around ten. He appreciates a lit fire and a prepared tea tray upon his arrival. The journey from the car park to the office tends to chill him.'

Evie blinked at Miss Whisker, a cloud of perplexity forming in her mind. 'Will I be performing this task?'

'Yes, yes,' said Miss Whisker. 'As the newest member of the typing pool, you'll be expected to come in early, light the fire and get the place warm for Mr Quill's arrival.'

Evie's thoughts raced. *Is this why I graduated first in my class? To be a skivvy?* She struggled to hide her rebellious reaction.

Miss Whisker, oblivious to the storm brewing in Evie's eyes, continued her monologue. 'After some time, you will be entrusted with the keys to this grand establishment and be expected to open up each morning. Once your tasks here are fulfilled, you can join the others in the typing pool.'

And without another word, Miss Whisker guided Evie out of the regal room, navigating a maze of corridors and through a set of swinging doors. Suddenly, Evie was engulfed by a cacophony of sound, standing in the heart of a cavernous office. The open space was organised into three rows of desks, each hosting a typist immersed in her task. The rhythmic clatter of typewriters was punctuated by the soft murmur of voices through their headphones.

Miss Whisker helped Evie off with her Sunday coat and arranged it on a hanger. Evie, meanwhile, gingerly lowered herself onto the chair at her designated desk. The nylon stockings she had on, unfamiliar and irritating against her skin, stirred yearnings for her summer freedom. Her tight pencil skirt rode up to her thighs, obliging her to tug it back into place, a lesson in modesty ingrained by the nuns at school. Her mother had insisted on purchasing a pale blue twinset for her new role, which, while not providing much warmth, certainly looked smart. She found solace in the faux string of pearls adorning her neck, a symbol of elegance she felt added some grace to her appearance.

In the week prior, Evie's mother and elder sister had journeyed to Dublin to help her settle in to her new flat on Leeson Street. She was to share the space with three other Galway girls – and lucky to get it, she was informed. But Evie struggled to see the luck in her situation. The flat was dank and cold. Condensation clogged up the windows and the tiled floor was chilly underfoot. Her bed was narrow, with a lumpy mattress and a worn candlewick bedspread. The pale green colour reminded her of something she'd rather not think about. By the time she squashed her few belongings into her wardrobe space, there was hardly room to breathe in the tiny quarters.

Time moved on, and Evie began to settle into the routine of her job. She got up at seven every morning, abluted in freezing water, pulled on her working clothes and walked around the corner to the office on Stephen's Green. A cleaner let her in, and she proceeded up the stairway to Mr Quill's office. Once there, her working habits were the same every day. She rolled up her sleeves and hunkered down to remove the still warm ashes from the grate, putting them into the metal bucket left there for the purpose. She rolled up some newspapers, put them in the grate, added some kindling and put a match to the pile.

Once the fire was lighting, she added a couple of logs and moved on to her second chore which was setting the tea tray. The large silver tray remained in place overnight, but the pink and white china was returned to the cabinet each evening. She set the tray, adding milk to the china jug, and making sure there were enough sugar lumps in the bowl. Once she had filled the plate with Marietta biscuits, Mr Quill's room was ready for his arrival. It was warm and cosy, such a contrast to her damp, little basement flat.

Evie often imagined Mr Quill sitting in the deep armchair by the fire, reading the *Financial Times* before his day began. She wondered what it would be like to be a man, to be educated and to have the devotion of a bevy of females looking after his every material need. Then, shaking away such thoughts, she would head to the bustling hive of the typing pool to commence her day's work.

The other girls in the typing pool were very friendly and they had great laughs at tea break in the common room or when they went out at lunchtime. The weather was still mild enough for them to have their sandwiches in Stephen's Green and Evie soon became acquainted with plenty of other young people, all up from the country, working in typing pools, or in the civil service offices nearby. Evie was almost happy. In the evenings, they went to occasional hops and dances in Earlsfort Terrace, but everybody went home at weekends.

The presence of Mr Quill seemed to permeate the entire office. His arrival each morning sparked a subtle current of anticipation.

Everyone walked by the doors of his office as though they were stepping on eggshells. In actuality, he was a quiet man, his mind often lost in the clouds, tangled up in matters of significance in distant lands. To Evie, he appeared shy and ill-at-ease amongst a sea of women. He interacted amiably with the young girls, extending his dictation politely and rarely dealing directly with them over errors. That responsibility fell upon the stalwart shoulders of Miss Whisker. She had no hesitation in highlighting mistakes, her stern demeanour enough to send tremors through the girls, amplifying their errors through sheer nervousness.

As the days flowed into one another, Evie began to sense a shift in her position. Miss Whisker and Mr Quill trusted her with more responsibilities, no longer treating her as the fledgling in the nest. The affirmation came when she was tasked with the responsibility of opening and closing the office. The additional burden left her torn between a sense of pride and apprehension, but she accepted the arrangement with grace.

Meanwhile, in the Leeson Street flat, the girls grappled with the onset of winter. There was nowhere to dry the clothes that they rinsed out in the hand basins and, of course, they wanted to always look their best – not necessarily for work but in the interests of their emerging social lives.

Each morning, Evie looked forward to the comforting warmth of Mr Quill's office fire before plunging into the bustling world of the typing pool. On one such morning, she had rinsed her stockings out overnight and they did not dry hanging on the chair by her bed. When it was time to put them on, she thought for a second, stuffed them into her coat pocket and headed off to work. Once in the warm office, she hung the stockings over the back of one of the chairs, pushed it towards the fire and had enough time to wait until they were dry.

Emboldened with this new idea, next day she brought in some knickers which were not quite dry and hung them on the chair as she busied herself with her morning chores. They were still damp when it was time for her to go to the typing pool, but she judged that later she could leave them there overnight and they would be dry by morning. Nobody else would see them, as she was first in and last out.

What a difference this innovation made to her life! In no time at all, she had worked out how to construct a small airing line in Mr Quill's office and had let some of the other girls in on the act. She set it up shortly before she left for home each evening, and by morning, everybody's smalls were crisp and dry.

However, one Wednesday morning threw her routine off balance. As she inserted her key into the front door's lock, she was met with an unexpected discovery – the door was already unlocked.

Panicked, she sprinted up the staircase to Mr Quill's office, only to find him surveying an impromptu laundry line of women's underwear in his office. His face flushed in embarrassment upon noticing her, while Evie, equally mortified, was at a loss for words.

Hastily, she dismantled the clothesline, stashed the offending items into her pockets and under her jumper, and without a word, beat a hasty retreat.

As tea breaks and lunchtime passed in a haze of anxiety, Evie felt certain her job was in jeopardy. Then, Miss Whisker delivered the dreaded message,

'Mr Quill would like to see you in his office.'

Evie approached the mahogany door like a convict awaiting her sentence.

At his summons, she entered, her eyes brimming with unshed tears.

'Evie,' Mr Quill began.

'Yes, Mr Quill. I'm so...' Evie's voice trembled.

He raised a hand to gently halt her words. 'Evie,' he began again, his voice softer this time. 'Perhaps it would be better if I take up the task of opening up the office in the mornings. I do appreciate your dedication and enthusiasm, but...'

Evie nodded, her throat feeling tight. She swallowed hard. 'I understand, Mr Quill. I apologise for any discomfort my actions may have caused.'

Mr Quill let out a chuckle, surprising Evie. His stern demeanour had softened, a glint of amusement in his eyes.

'I'll admit it was a surprise,' he confessed. 'But no harm done. You're a valuable member of our team, Evie. Don't let this incident overshadow that.'

Evie's First Job

    Relief washed over Evie, her worries dissipating with Mr Quill's understanding words. Perhaps, she mused, life at Andrew Quill Solicitors wouldn't be as stern and solemn as she'd first thought. Maybe, there was room for a bit of humour amidst the mountains of legal briefs and the cacophony of typewriters.

International Adventures

The Real Africa

We departed from the hotel in Lusaka early on Saturday morning with light overnight bags, plenty of bottled water and one classical music tape, Mozart's *Concerto for Bassoon and Orchestra in B Flat Major*.

'These business trips aren't so bad after all,' said Christine.

There is no doubt that our work at the time allowed for interesting weekends. Our trips to Lusaka often spanned two full weeks, leaving a free weekend in between. Although very enjoyable, the work was pressured, not leaving much opportunity for winding down in the evenings. When we discovered that we also had a bank holiday attached to our weekend, we were raring to go.

Colleagues who had been in Lusaka before us raved about Victoria Falls. Ignoring the small matter of an eight-hour car journey, Christine and I decided to go for it.

Brimming with anticipation, we set out on Saturday morning. Adventurers in search of new experiences, new sights, new sounds, we were looking for the Real Africa.

We were familiar with the peripheral roads, having been around to the airport and to some of the outlying areas, so getting out of Lusaka and on to the Kafue Road was not so difficult.

Christine and I planned to share the driving and I took the first stint. We passed through

Mazabuka and Monza without stopping. We had been advised that the logical place to take a break was at Choma, halfway through our journey. There we could find a light snack, freshen up and be on our way.

The word 'pothole' in Zambia really means crater. The dry road blew sand up in front of us, making it almost impossible to see the next pothole ahead. The car rattled and jerked along a road that seemed to have no end, and we chatted nervously as we drove. Mozart was our only distraction and even that grew tiresome after a while.

At last, we reached our halfway stop at Choma. Our intrepid hearts sank when we saw the town that we had been looking forward to exploring. It was a sandy track, lined on either side by dusty shacks and ramshackle buildings. We drove down one side of the street, turned, and drove up the other side, eventually seeing a building advertising snacks and cold beer. We parked outside, gathered our bundles of kwacha together and went indoors.

Inside, the noise of the ceiling fan was the only sound to be heard. A shaft of sunlight beamed dust motes to the floor. We looked towards what we supposed to be the Reception and saw the soles of a pair of feet upon the desk. On further investigation, there was a young man attached to these feet by a pair of long legs. The rest of his body was seated in a decrepit office chair on the other side of the desk.

Timidly, we woke him up. He stirred to his feet and we asked him if we could get some lunch.

'Oh no, I am so sorry. No lunch, no lunch Saturday. Only drinks, Madam, only drinks.'

Christine and I looked at each other in dismay. We had not bothered to pack a picnic. All we had was water. However, we were here, and needed to at least regain our composure before moving on.

The day was bright, the sun was high, and we asked if we could have our drinks outside. The young man was agreeable to this and showed us out into the beer garden. A series of small semi-circular stone walls which acted as seats adjoined small stone tables. As there was nobody there except us, we picked the nearest one.

After an interminable time, the young man returned with two large brown bottles of Mosi beer, the local brew. This was not the lunch we anticipated but we determined to make the best of it. Christine, who smoked at the time, produced a Marlboro Lite pack with one remaining cigarette, and a yellow lighter. She lit the cigarette, leaving the crushed packet and lighter on the table.

'This place reminds me of that saying about watches and time,' I said to Christine.

'What was that?'

'When God made the world, he gave time to the Africans and watches to the Europeans!'

Christine laughed.

'Do you need to get more cigarettes?' I enquired.

'No, I'm giving them up for good, from this day on.'

We drank long thirsty drafts from our beer and decided to ignore this first hiccup of our wonderful adventure.

Leaving a few kwachas on the table outside, we paid the sleepy boy at the reception for our drinks and left.

Back on the road, hungry and a little anxious now, we continued our progress along the old, pitted road. The second half of the journey was more hazardous than the first. Even in the middle of nowhere there were people with loaded packs walking on the sides of the road, and we knew of the dangers of unexpected wildlife. We weren't too surprised when an elephant suddenly appeared and crossed the road in front of us.

We were exhausted and getting irritable.

'Can't you play something else?' demanded Christine. 'I am so sick of that bassoon!'

It was getting dark as, with some relief, we arrived at the town of Livingstone. This was just a border bridge away from the Zimbabwean town of Victoria Falls.

It didn't help when I hit a traffic cone, sending it flying and causing much more alarm than necessary. We heard the screeching brakes of a large Land Rover. Its occupant jumped out and we realised with alarm that he was armed. He was an exceptionally large official and made for a scary spectacle in his bushranger clothing. In a strong South African accent, he lectured us on the dangers of two young ladies driving alone in the dark and potentially causing traffic accidents.

Suitably chastened, we made our way to our recommended budget accommodation. It was clean, with no frills. Thankfully, they were still expecting us. Exhausted, we put our heads down and never stirred until breakfast next morning.

A new day dawned!

The Victoria Falls, the largest sheet of falling water in the world, exceeded our wildest imaginings. We bathed in the constant mist coming off the water. The fine spray caused a perpetual rainbow and turned the surrounding area into a full-blown tropical forest.

The water roared as it fell over the cliff and down into the Zambezi River below. The local people call the waterfall Mosi-O-Tunya or the noise that thunders.

Marvelling at the natural wonders surrounding us, Christine and I 'high fived' and agreed that this, at last, was the Real Africa.

Sunday came and an even bigger adventure was in store – white water rafting on the Zambezi River.

We were overcome by exhilaration as we faced into the highs and lows of the rapids which, if we weren't careful, would eventually take us straight over the Victoria Falls.

'What would our families at home think about this if they found out?' we speculated.

'I promised that I wouldn't do anything too dangerous!' screamed Christine.

To end the day, we travelled in a jeep to a Safari lodge with a view sloping down to a watering hole. Animals in abundance came there to have their evening drink.

Intoxicated by the African sunset, Christine toasted me with her gin and tonic, exclaiming: 'Here's to the Real Africa!'

By bedtime we were exhausted and not looking forward to the journey back to Lusaka in the morning. However, we were up at dawn, and organised a packed lunch to take with us on the road. The journey in full daylight was less intimidating and we arrived at Choma at midday.

'Will the town be any busier than it was on Friday?' I asked my companion hopefully.

It didn't seem like it. The lure of the familiar brought us straight back to the snack bar where we had stopped before. At least we knew what it was like.

We were greeted again by the noise of the ceiling fan.

'Look!' I whispered to Christine, giggling.

The soles of a pair of white trainers rested on the desk. The same young man, attached to the feet by his long legs and long body, woke up abruptly when we tried to get his attention.

Today we only wanted drinks and we made our way out to wait in the beer garden with a little more confidence than on our previous visit. In front of us was the same array of small semi-circular stone walls serving as seating, adjoining small stone tables.

On the table nearest to us, the one we'd used on Friday, were two empty Mosi bottles, one crushed Marlboro Lite package, one yellow lighter, and a few kwachas.

We glanced at each other and started to laugh.

'Christine,' I said. 'We travelled all that way to find the Real Africa and it was here all the time!'

Another Mouth to Feed

On a world map, Zambia resembles a butterfly, with wings spread across the central southern plain. The country is land-locked and heavily reliant on agriculture since the demise of the copper industry.

In the mid-1990s, the Irish Department of Foreign Affairs had a bilateral aid agreement with the Zambian government. As a minor public servant, I found myself in Lusaka with no relevant experience and a report to file on 'Women in Agriculture in Zambia'.

Mrs Banda, my guide, was a force of nature. She had set herself up as an advocate for the poorest, most deprived inhabitants of the country – village women. Tall and broad, she dressed in brightly coloured florals with her hair swept up into a matching turban. Armed with startling, red-rimmed glasses and very large hoop earrings, she exuded authority and power. From a relatively well-off background herself, she had dedicated her life to the cause of women in villages in Zambia.

In an effort to break the cycle of poverty, she set herself up to deliver 'microcredit', providing small loans to village women to help them grow crops. It was her view that providing agricultural training to local people, thereby helping them to produce better crops with higher yields, would improve food security for everyone.

To begin with, she briefed me with some background information. I learned that in many remote Zambian villages, life is a cruel and meaningless cycle of suffering and poverty. Although there are many reasons for this, undoubtedly a low level of education is a major factor. In the main, women perform the daily chores, childrearing, and any subsistence farming. The men sit back, drink beer and pursue more manly activities.

Mrs Banda had a dream for the women in her programme. She wanted each of them to become self-sufficient in food production for their families. This would be achieved by lending each woman a small amount of cash to buy maize seed. No longer would they have to purchase the maize meal that formed the staple of their diet, *'nshima*. Once planted and harvested, part of the yield could be held back to feed the family for the winter. Any surplus would be taken to the market and sold. The money realised should be sufficient to pay back the loan and purchase more seed for the coming year.

Before any of this could happen, a complex series of negotiations had to take place with the local Chief. The patriarchal nature of the society dictated that women couldn't own property and Mrs Banda had to persuade the Chief to give women plots of their own. Then they had to get some rudimentary training before collecting their 'seed capital'.

Mrs Banda and I set off together on a field trip to Chongwe, 15km south-east of Lusaka. We were going to meet Bupe Mulenge, a client of Mrs Banda's. The local Chief had given Bupe a plot of land and she had embarked on her farming career with great enthusiasm. Today's mission was to get an update on her situation and collect the money outstanding from her loan.

I soon discovered that Zambian roads are rough and potholed. In the wet season, rain washes the roads out, making them muddy and very difficult to travel on. People in the villages do not have cars so they walk along the roads, sometimes for days on end.

In Chongwe town, we saw the market, a collection of lean-to shacks and dilapidated stores strung along the road. The women, straight-backed and straight-legged, sat in the sun on reed mats thrown on the sand. Stalls of rickety tables held meagre pyramids of onions, tomatoes, bananas, okra, pumpkin leaves and peanuts, watched over by the women who planted, grew, weeded and watered each plant.

As we travelled, Mrs Banda told me something of Bupe's life. A normal day might begin at five o'clock in the morning, when she swept the surroundings of her compound – an activity that could affect her respiratory system unless she reduced the dust by sprinkling the ground with water at the same time.

Between 6am and 9am, she drew water from a stream about two kilometres away. Her containers, transported on her head, carried between 10 and 20 litres. She made five daily trips in order to draw enough water for the whole household.

In the afternoon, she spent three hours fetching heavy loads of firewood. This was not a straight-forward task. Uncontrolled cutting of trees in the Chimtende ward, where she lived, had denuded the land. Bupe had to walk long distances, past scattered shreds of shrubs, in order to find wood suitable for the fire.

In addition, she did all the other household chores – feeding her offspring, cooking, bathing, and doing the laundry. Her husband didn't help with any of these activities.

In spite of this, Bupe was an enthusiastic participant in Mrs Banda's programme. She didn't seem to mind the extra work involved in planting and tending her crop.

Shortly before we reached the village, we noticed a woman waving at the side of the road.

'That's Bupe,' said Mrs Banda. 'I wonder why she didn't wait in the village as we agreed?'

We pulled over and got out of the car. The Zambian women greeted each other. I hung back, waiting to be introduced. But I could see that Bupe was distraught. Sobbing bitterly as she embraced Mrs Banda, she began to tell her a long story. I couldn't understand one word.

Mrs Banda invited Bupe to sit into the car, and amid gulps of water and shuddering sobs, she recounted her experience. The story had to be translated for me, as we made our way back to Lusaka.

Apparently, Bupe found participation in the programme difficult from the beginning, largely due to her husband's attitude. He resented the fact that she had been given the plot – not that he wanted anything to do with it. He hated her new independence, fearing he was losing control. He constantly castigated her for being too tired after her day's work to be, as he put it, a proper wife to her husband.

Bupe tolerated his abuse, knowing that her larger goal of becoming self-sufficient in maize was within her grasp. She tended her little crop diligently and when harvest time came, she proudly reaped what she had sown. Once the freshly milled seeds were bagged, she put enough aside to feed the family for the winter. With that, she still had two bags left and she prepared to take them to Chongwe Market.

Her husband had other ideas. He announced that a woman's place was at home and that no wife of his would go to sell at the market. He would do it himself.

So, early in the morning on the designated day, he set off from the village with the two bags hoisted on his back.

The sun was setting when he returned. Bupe heard the children clamouring and came out of her hut. She saw her husband approaching. A young woman, a stranger, walked by his side.

Unable to control her excitement, Bupe ran towards him, shouting: 'Did you sell our grain? Were the people pleased with the quality? Can I have my money to give Mrs Banda?'

His reply filled her heart with despair.

'I have no money for you,' he said. 'All these hard months you have not been a good wife to me. When I sold the grain, I bought a new wife, a younger one, who would not be tired all the time like you are. Agatha, say hello to Bupe'.

Bupe's dream of a better life for herself and her children evaporated on his alcohol laden breath.

Mary Rose Tobin

'And so, Mrs Banda', she concluded, 'I have no money to repay my loan'.

The Secret

No matter how much we complained about traveling steerage, our project manager wouldn't pay for business class. The flight to Lusaka was, as usual, uncomfortable, and boring. I was allocated a middle seat, squashed between a sumo wrestler and a mother breastfeeding her twins, so there was no getting up once I was seated. My travelling companion and colleague, Alice, wasn't the greatest of company. She sat as far away from me as possible, where I couldn't see her, and we had little opportunity for conversation or chat. I resigned myself to a long sleepless night.

We landed without problems after the eight-hour flight and emerged into the strong sunlight of Lusaka Airport. I blinked and stumbled, assailed by the whiteness of the walls and the smell of the heat rising off the tarmac. Immigration went smoothly. A mere twenty minutes after landing, we met up with our local hosts, Agatha and Colliard, who were patiently waiting for us in the bustling arrivals area.

I had forgotten how confusing and chaotic Lusaka is, with its unplanned neighbourhoods and streets. Once inside the city limits, we sped past the busy stores and shopping centres lining Cairo Road to check in at the Pamodzi Hotel. This was to be our home and our workplace for the next two weeks.

When we arrived, Colliard showed us where the project car was parked and at our disposal. I held onto the keys, as Alice said she didn't intend driving. We all arranged to meet at 8:30 next morning in the hotel training suite. Alice and I checked into the hotel. We exchanged room numbers, but I didn't bother remembering hers, as she would inevitably change it. I had worked with her abroad before, and knew she always found something wrong with the first room she was allocated! We arranged to meet in the restaurant for lunch. I was glad to have time to unwind and freshen up.

We had a decent barbecue in the restaurant and spent the afternoon at the pool. When it came to dinner, I was in the mood to have a couple of drinks and go to bed early. Alice waved away the wine list, drank only water, and excused herself before dessert. So, this was to be my company for a fortnight!

At breakfast next morning, Alice mentioned she'd slept badly and asked me to run the first training session. I didn't mind. I loved the challenge of meeting a room full of strangers who would turn into friends as the week progressed. Zambian people are formal, and almost excessively polite. We had been well briefed about the more obvious cultural differences and were watchful of falling into any pitfalls. The only gaffe I remember from that first morning is enquiring about the whereabouts of a Mr Banda, whose name was on our list.

'I'm afraid he is late,' one of his colleagues explained. The gentleman never arrived, and I subsequently learned that he was recently deceased. He really was 'the late' Mr Banda.

We got off to a good start, and the working days passed quickly. Alice, who seemed to have sleeping difficulties, always asked to take the later sessions, so I needed to be bright and alert each morning. Since we never sat up late, this wasn't a problem. Our group was enthusiastic and full of curiosity about the way things were done in the Irish public service. I believe they learned something from us during the training sessions, but nowhere near as much as we learned from these polite, gentle people.

Just as well our days were busy because the evenings were rather dull. I missed my normal access to the internet and my various other technological distractions. I quickly learned that there was no point suggesting a night out, or even a bottle of wine at dinner. Alice always seemed in a hurry to go to her room and was evasive when I asked her what she planned to do. I imagined that she missed her husband and perhaps tried to phone him in the evenings. They had been through some difficult years and I sensed a sadness lying just below the surface.

I persuaded her to come with me to Lilayi Lodge for the weekend, as a reward to ourselves for working so hard during the week. This well-known game lodge is about 20km from Lusaka and off the beaten track.

After driving about 5km down a dirt road, we came to the electronic gates of the complex. We knew from the promotional material that the expansive grounds were home to many different species of antelope. With no predators in the vicinity, visitors were able to wander around safely, marvelling at the abundance of giraffe, zebra, kudu, roan, hartebeest, and more.

We laughed at the quaint guinea fowl that puttered about everywhere as we navigated the driveway to the reception area. Once we had settled into our 'rooms' – a little hut each, but well equipped and quite adequate – we sat on the outside deck overlooking the waterhole. Guidebook in hand, we watched a family of zebra and identified some warthog and waterbuck coming for their evening refreshment. I had a few 'sundowners' just watching the animals, and then we went to the restaurant for dinner. While we were eating, the lawn outside the restaurant filled up with more grazing deer. I was spellbound, never having imagined that watching wildlife in an African sunset could be such an extraordinary experience.

The meal on that Saturday evening was excellent and the wine list comprehensive. I chose a local red, and thanks to the attentive waiter I never had to wait for a refill. Alice, as usual, stuck with water and remained quiet and pensive.

When the meal was over, I still had some wine in my glass, so I persuaded Alice to sit with me on the lawn to enjoy the sounds and smells of the African night. It was pitch dark, although the sky was scattered with stars. The air was replete with the scents of perfumed hibiscus and jasmine, and noisy with unidentifiable animal and insect sounds. Mindful of the mosquitoes, we both wore long trousers and long-sleeved tops. Any exposed areas were well sprayed, and we hoped we wouldn't be bitten. Since we were required to take anti-malaria medication each day, we weren't overly worried about this occupational hazard.

We sat quietly, chatting, until suddenly I jumped up with a start.

'Alice!' I shouted. 'An insect just flew into my ear!'

She looked at me in disbelieving horror.

'Help me, help me!' I stuttered. 'It's in my eardrum! I can hear it flying around inside my ear! It's inside my head!'

'Calm down,' she snapped authoritatively. 'Let me have a look.'

In the pitch dark, this didn't make much sense. I was almost hysterical as I leaned my ear towards her.

'Listen,' I cried. 'Can you hear it?'

She placed her ear on mine, and straightening up, took a deep breath.

'Stay here,' she commanded. 'I have something in my room that will help.'

Moving quickly, she soon returned, carrying a half-full Smirnoff bottle.

'Stay still,' she barked. 'I'll just pour some of this in. It will disinfect your ear and kill the insect.'

Firmly, she held my head and tipped some of the liquid into my ear. The insect noise subsided and finally ceased.

'It stopped,' I said tentatively. 'But that means it's dead inside my head.'

'Never mind that,' she said. 'At least it died happy. We'll go to a doctor when we get back to Lusaka.'

It was only when I calmed down in bed later that I wondered why Alice just happened to have a half-full bottle of vodka in her room.

Mr Boopathy

Mr Boopathy navigated across the busy street and turned his taxi into the narrow lane at the side of the hotel. With practised agility, he guided his car over the dusty potholes. Glad of the brief respite from the sun's rays, he crawled along, careful not to damage the paintwork on his gleaming Toyota, his pride and joy. He emerged into the crowded car park at the rear of the Taj Hotel. Greeting his fellow drivers, he stripped off his blue shirt. It had absorbed his sweat all day. Now it lay in a damp heap on the front seat of the car. Then he removed the white calico seat covers, made a bundle of the clothes, and filled the basin with water.

This was the part of the day he most enjoyed. His friend, Raju, gave him a cool bottle of water. He scrubbed his laundry and chatted about the events of the day.

'Tomorrow,' said Boopathy, 'I start a two-week service.'

'Lucky bastard,' said Raju. 'A two-week commission is rare enough these days. Where is he from?'

'They,' corrected Boopathy. 'A couple from New York.'

'Business? Or tourists?' asked Raju.

'A bit of both, I think,' answered Boopathy. 'He has family roots in Tamil Nadu, and she wants to see the sights! Retired, I think.'

'Oh! You are a lucky bastard, Boo! Plenty of American dollars, yes? You will be extra nice to them, yes?'

'I'm always nice.'

'You are, Boo! Even with the worst of them, you manage to keep your patience. I don't know how you do it. Sometimes I could scream at the things those people ask me to do. They look at us as if we are inferior... as if we are beneath them. Westerners!'

'Now, Raju, you can't live your life in hate. Make the best of what you've got. Everyone has troubles. It doesn't matter whether you are rich or poor.'

Boopathy was at Bangalore Airport bright and early the next morning. The flight from New York was delayed but he remained at his post, holding up the sign that said, 'George and Ruby Patterson'. When the crowds started to spill out from the Arrivals area, Boo stood on tiptoe and elbowed his way to the front barrier. He was not going to get off on the wrong foot with his new clients.

A red-haired lady of indeterminate age, wearing a bright yellow sundress, emerged. Her sunglasses were perched on top of her head and her red lipstick shone, but it was her loud voice that made her stand out. Following in her wake was a man of similar age, wheeling a trolley laden with suitcases. He wore a Panama hat and a heavy business suit. With his harassed eyes, he cast worried glances, first ahead to the Arrivals area and then back to his unencumbered wife.

'George and Ruby Patterson,' shouted Boo. 'Over here! Over here!'

'Oh, look, George! There's our porter,' said the woman. 'Leave the cases. Let this Indian look after them from here.'

George stopped in his tracks.

'I think I should bring them at least as far as the exit,' he began.

'Nonsense!' the woman snapped. 'You-Whooo! You-Whooo! Over here, Boy. Over here, you foolish man. Can you not see us? He cannot see us, George. Shout at him!'

'Give the man a chance, dear. He's blocked by the barrier. We have to go through this exit before he can reach us.'

The woman sucked in her cheeks and scowled. She took off at pace towards the exit barrier.

'Come along, George,' she shouted. 'Don't dally!'

Boopathy expertly removed the trolley from George's hands. 'I am Mr Boopathy,' he said as he shook the Pattersons' hands warmly and asked them to follow him to the car.

'Can't you bring the car to the door?' demanded Ruby. 'I'm exhausted after that long flight, and I can't walk another step.'

Boopathy demurred politely. 'No, Mrs Patterson, that, I am afraid, is not permitted'.

Ruby walked sulkily to the car park, moaning all the while about the heat and the smell.

It did not take Boopathy long to get the measure of the Americans who would be his constant companions for the next ten days. It was clear that Ruby gave the orders and George snapped to attention. He would have to be on his guard.

Their journey would take them from Bangalore to Kochi via the Nilgiri Hills, taking in a combination of cultural sites, wildlife, local life, and beautiful scenery. The Pattersons would stay in a new hotel every night. Each leg of the journey was carefully planned in advance and there was a lot of ground to cover.

Mr Boopathy was an excellent driver and did his best to be good company. Each morning he was at the hotel reception at the appointed time, in a freshly washed uniform blue shirt. He kept the interior of the car immaculate. The white calico seat covers were changed daily, and fresh bottles of water appeared as if by magic.

Ruby's bad temper and disdain for her surroundings were compensated for by George's pleasant manner. When he wasn't jumping to attention and tending to his wife's demands, however trivial, he bombarded Boopathy with questions. To begin with, Boopathy wasn't giving too much away. It took George a while to acquire the information that their Indian guide was married, with a 21-year-old daughter and a ten-year-old son.

At the end of each day, the threesome parted company after checking in to the latest hotel. In the early days of the trip, George was uncomfortable at the idea that Boopathy was alone for the long evenings and invited him to dinner.

'What can you be thinking, George?' bickered Ruby. 'The servants can't eat with us!'

She need not have worried. The invitation embarrassed Boopathy, and he politely refused, saying he preferred to eat and sleep with the other drivers. George assumed that there were staff quarters somewhere in the hotels. When he found out that all the drivers slept in their cars and ate at the local 'thattukada' – a covered cart parked by a roadside, selling local street food, and frequented by local men – he was mortified.

Nothing would do George but to visit a thattukada and see for himself. Mr Boopathy was not happy about this.

'I phoned Mrs Boopathy and told her what you wanted to do,' he said. 'And she also does not think it a good idea'. But he gamely escorted George there despite his misgivings – and it was quite a dining experience! George thought it the highlight of the entire tour. Ruby showed no interest, opting to stay back and have the hairdresser come to her room instead.

A couple of days into the trip, Mr Boopathy and George were momentarily alone. Boopathy used the opportunity to make a request. 'Perhaps,' he said, 'you don't need all the toiletries supplied by the hotel each day? And if not, and if you don't mind, could you give them to me to bring to the orphanage?'

George didn't mind; he and Ruby had plenty. But the orphanage?

When George told this to Ruby, she was outraged.

'Orphanage?' she snorted. 'Garbage! The guy wants them for his wife and daughter!'

For once, George ignored her, and next day, he left the small bottles of shampoo, shower gel and conditioner in the side pocket of the back seat. He told Mr Boopathy just to look there every day, and he would leave what he could. It became their little secret.

Once into the Nilgiri Hills, the temperatures dropped very noticeably, and George worried about Mr Boopathy sleeping in his car. He would be very cold, he thought. To Ruby's intense irritation, he wandered up and down the street market to find Boopathy a fleece blanket. When he presented it to him, it was accepted graciously, but again with obvious embarrassment.

As the journey progressed, Mr Boopathy became chattier and more responsive to George's curious questioning.

'Why don't you tell me a bit more about your family?' he asked.

'I will show you my beautiful daughter!' Boopathy replied proudly, taking out his phone and scrolling through his photos until he found what he was looking for. Beaming from the upturned screen was a glamorous young woman in graduate's cap and gown, with Boopathy on one side and a lady, who must have been her mother, on the other.

'She has just completed her master's degree in HR and is now looking for employment.'

'There's a coincidence!' said George. 'She has the same qualification as you, Rubes!'

Ruby studiously examined her fingernails. Yes, she also had a master's degree in HR. It was superior, of course, to anything an Indian girl might have.

'Clever as well as beautiful!' exclaimed George. 'Is it usual for girls in South India to be so well educated?'

Boopathy's face darkened.

'No,' he said. 'Many girls in South India must put up with discrimination, prejudice, violence and neglect all their lives, whether they are single or married women. It is difficult for them to get a good education unless they come from a wealthy family.'

'As a matter of fact,' he went on, 'my daughter is adopted. My wife and I decided that we would take a girl from the orphanage and give her a chance in life that she would not have otherwise. She has been a wonderful daughter to us.'

He paused and was quiet for a moment.

'I support her in her decision not to marry right away, but to make a career for herself, even though this is most unusual in our family.'

He sighed.

'My own mother will just have to get used to this.'

George asked no more questions that day, and Ruby was uncharacteristically quiet.

Towards the end of the tour, the itinerary took in a visit to the Redemptorist school in Koonoor where George's father had been a pupil before the First World War. Ruby and George were surrounded by excitable boys and girls, just about to break up for their winter holiday. The students chattered in passable English, each with a torrent of questions about life in New York.

'Let us have some selfies with you!' they demanded.

When the journey recommenced, George asked Mr Boopathy to tell him more about his son.

'He is almost ten years old,' he replied. 'As a matter of fact, it's his birthday next week.'

'Oh,' George said. 'Will you have a party for him?'

'No,' Boopathy replied. 'On his birthday every year, we have a special family tradition.'

'What's that?' enquired George.

'Well, we collect together the ingredients to make a big meal, and we go as a family to the orphanage and cook for the children,' replied Boopathy. 'It is my way of showing my son how fortunate he is. He comes from a loving family and will have many chances in life. Why should he party while other children go hungry?'

'Did you do that last year?' asked George. 'Do you have a photo we can see?'

'Sure,' said Boopathy, producing his phone with a flourish. 'Here is my wife, my daughter, my son and some of the orphanage children.'

George was fascinated by this insight into Boopathy's family life and looked at Ruby for her reaction. She wouldn't believe a word, he thought. He was surprised to see her dabbing at her eyes with a tissue.

That evening over dinner, George was a bit worried about his unusually subdued wife.

'What's the matter, Rubes?' he cajoled. 'Sad that tomorrow's our last day?'

'No,' she said quietly. 'I'm sad that I didn't believe Boopathy about the toiletries for the orphanage.'

Next day at the airport, George studied his wife carefully. She politely thanked Mr Boopathy for holding the car door open for her.

They had agreed at breakfast on a generous tip for Boopathy. Ruby handed him not one but two envelopes at the Departures Gate.

'Mr Boopathy,' she said. 'I thank you with all my heart for your company on this journey. You have been knowledgeable and polite. You were always prepared to go the extra mile to make our days as full and interesting as possible.'

She lowered her eyes and scuffed her feet on the dusty floor. Then she looked up at Boopathy.

'Through you,' she went on, 'I learned the most unexpected things, and not always about India. Thank you, I will never forget you.'

George was puzzled. As they passed through Departures, he quizzed Ruby.

'Two envelopes? What was in the second one?'

'Oh, just a little something for the boy's birthday party.'

The Foundlings

Arise!

The dormitory in the Foundling Hospital had enough beds for fifty girls. Each bed was occupied tonight. Lucy slept fitfully. She tossed and turned, listening to the collective heaving of the many sleeping bodies, interspersed with snores and other nocturnal sounds.

Lucy was nine years old and had been sleeping in this dormitory since she was five. When her eyelids drooped, and she succumbed to heavy drowsiness, memories of happier days flooded her mind.

She imagined that she was in her foster home, sitting in the nook by the warm fire, untangling balls of wool for her foster mother. Every now and then, Mother sent a few words of praise her way. Lucy was all tucked up in her winter woollies. The aroma of baking bread filled the room. Wood smoke billowed from the chimney to create a warm blanket all around her. She was so happy; she could have burst. She was doing something useful. Mother was pleased with her. And she was loved.

In the background, she heard a church bell ringing. The sound was far away. She imagined herself levitating from her seat and floating up to the ceiling. Somehow, she passed through the ceiling. Now she was over the roof of the house. She was flying towards the church steeple. The sound of the bells grew louder and louder. She was so close to them now. Ding. Dong. She wanted to reach out and touch them. To feel the vibrations. To embrace the sound. She wanted to be as one with the bells. She wanted to be as one with the music.

'Wake up! Wake up!' shouted Polly, disrupting the serenity of Lucy's reverie.

The rude clamour of the morning bell and Polly's urgings awakened her, jolting her out of her sleep and into the cold dormitory.

Polly was shaking her. Vigorously.

'Wake up, Lucy! You have to help me. We can't be late for breakfast.'

Lucy rubbed her eyes. Then stretched.

Poor Polly! Always anxious and fretful. Lucy watched the other girls spilling out of their beds. Scratching. Yawning. Soon the tranquil dormitory became a hurly-burly of activity. A teeming throng of bodies, swarming in various stages of undress.

'Now, now, little one,' said Lucy, loud above the commotion. 'Don't worry! Look, I'm wide awake! I'll be dressed before you, I'll bet!'

Polly ran to her own bed. She struggled into her scratchy, brown dress. Then, she pulled on her apron and white cap.

'Can you help me with this?'

Lucy's heart melted at the sight of the little girl holding out a tippet in her little white hands. Polly just couldn't get the knack of arranging the shoulders of her uniform correctly.

Lucy couldn't resist teasing her a little.

'When will you ever learn to arrange that tippet properly? One of these days, you'll be caught with saggy shoulders and then what will happen?'

'Oh, please Lucy, help me!'

'Of course I will, pet. Come here and sit down.'

Polly sat on the edge of Lucy's bed. When the tippet had been arranged, Lucy helped the little girl to pull on the stiff, darned stockings and heavy boots that completed her ensemble.

'There you are, my sweet pet. All dolled up in your finery! The prettiest little Polly in the whole of London town!'

Lift Up Your Heads

Photograph: Sophia Anderson, *Foundling Girls in the Chapel* © Coram in the care of The Foundling Museum

Lucy was turning into a beautiful girl. She was tall for her age, with a pale complexion, and flawless skin. Even the ugly, brown uniform dress could not hide her developing figure. Her light blue eyes seemed to reveal her soul. She was kind by nature, but possessed a fiery spirit. This would stand to her throughout her life.

When she was re-admitted to the Foundling Hospital at age five, her hair had been shorn. This was the practice in the hospital to prevent the spread of headlice. It took years for her hair to regain its bounce and early sheen. Tucked up under her cap, it added a waifish air to her already dreamy demeanour.

She remembered how distraught she was when she was brought to the hospital. Her foster mother had been so kind. Separating from her was an ordeal and a huge wrench for Lucy. She cried constantly. Had it not been for the kindness shown to her by an older girl, Hester, she would have disintegrated.

Lucy was eternally grateful to Hester. She determined that the best way to repay the kindness shown to her, was to do the same for another child whenever she could. So, when little Polly appeared, all red-eyed and tearful, Lucy immediately took her under her wing. She was happy to show the same kindness that had been shown to her to this needy, little girl. Poor Polly, as cute as a button. Her long lashes were always wet with tears. Nothing ever went her way. She clung like a limpet to her new big 'sister'. Lucy didn't mind.

The children attended daily service at the chapel, and went twice on Sundays. Girls and boys were together for services, though they were seated separately. No contact was supposed to take place between them. But the rules were there to be broken. Surreptitious notes were passed from hand to hand, secret liaisons were planned, innocent love affairs were hatched and plotted. Girls giggled. Boys strutted. The natural laws of attraction led to many an innocent caper. The stakes were even higher because it was forbidden. Those who were caught in companionship were invariably punished. But nothing could stop the hypnotic magnetism between boys and girls. At times, it was the only flicker of light in an otherwise dreary and gloomy existence.

That and music.

For Lucy, music had begun to take on a passion that elevated her from the mundaneness of her everyday existence. And it was in the chapel that she could exult in her burgeoning talents for expressing herself through song. The hospital chapel was an airy building, intended to impress and awe its patrons. It had solid substantial mahogany pews, vaulted balconies and beautiful, stained-glass windows. In the centre was a lofty, immovable marble pulpit. It was decorated throughout with tiles and had an astonishing acoustic. This House of God was designed to delight the eye and lift the spirits of all who entered. Nobody was immune from the majesty of its architecture and the atmosphere affected everyone who ventured into its sacred embrace. A mystical aura was felt by the governors, visitors, staff and foundlings alike.

The Foundling staff was very proud of the history of the hospital. On many occasions, Lucy had heard about the famous writer, who had helped to raise funds for the hospital when it was first founded. He had written *Oliver Twist*, the story of an orphan boy with no parents to care for him. The character of Tattycoram in *Little Dorrit* had his imagined childhood in the Foundling Hospital.

Oliver Twist and *Little Dorrit* were among the favourite stories read in the schoolroom. The children were told that Mr Dickens had rented a pew in the Hospital Chapel, and Lucy tried to make this seat her special place to sit.

But other girls wanted to sit in that place as well. Lucy had many friends, but she had enemies as well.

Lift Up Your Heads

There was a lot of jealousy amongst the girls. Three had reason to be jealous of Lucy.

Sarah resented her prowess at choir
Hetty resented her academic excellence.
Jenny resented her good looks

Sarah, the ringleader, could often be manipulative and try to sneak in offensive comments, doing everything she could to make other people dislike Lucy. She regularly told fibs about her and tried to ruin things for her. Naturally, she saved her meanness for when adults weren't looking.

These three formed a clique that made Lucy and Polly feel excluded.

Any time Lucy confronted her, Sarah claimed she was making things up. 'You're imagining things,' she'd say, and the other girls would laugh. Loony Lucy and Puny Polly were the horrible nicknames that they were given. These spiteful hurtful names were used many times every day.

Lucy knew that she had to be strong, not only for herself, but for the sake of the little girl as well.

'Hold your head high, Polly. Remember you're a beloved Child of God. I'm not going to let them ruin my life, and neither must you,' she would say to her friend.

The singing lessons during the week, where the children stood in line and sang the long dreary hymns were Lucy's favourite daytime interludes. Some of the girls hated this, but she loved going to the beautiful chapel. Even when Sarah, Hetty and Jane sang silly rhymes featuring Lucy's name, when they should have been singing their hymns, Lucy could rise above their nonsense and lose herself in the music.

At first, she could only hum uncertainly along with the piano music but as her confidence grew, so did her skill. Before long, she could make her voice soar high above the others.

Everyone knew that Mr Handel had been an early benefactor, that was why, every Christmas, *The Messiah* with an orchestra and chorus was performed in the chapel. The performance was for the Board of Governors and an invited audience of dignitaries drawn from London's high society. Lucy had made such progress that she was selected to join the chorus. This was a huge honour because usually only the older girls were chosen.

On Christmas day, Lucy awoke shivering and feverish. Every movement was painful. In tears, she struggled to put on her ugly, brown, serge dress. Her throat felt as if it were on fire. Hester saw her plight. She called Matron.

'It's off to the Infirmary with you, my girl.'

'But I have to sing,' croaked Lucy. 'Today is the most important day of my life!'

The concert went ahead without her. Lucy was devastated. For a long time afterwards, she was off her food and seemed to be losing her strength. She became more and more despondent. Even the pleas of Hester and Polly fell on deaf ears.

Then, one morning, Mrs Hackshaw announced a plan that might restore Lucy back to well-being. An artist had asked to visit the hospital. Her name was Sophie Gingembre. She had requested to borrow some girls to act as models for her paintings. The girls had to have interesting faces and personalities.

Mrs Hackshaw immediately thought of Lucy. This painting might distract her from her disappointment at not being able to sing on Christmas Day. It might be the very thing to bring her around. Imagine her surprise when Lucy said: 'I will pose for the painting. But Polly must be part of it too please. It's both of us, or none of us!'

Mrs Hackshaw acquiesced to the request. Secretly, she admired Lucy's spirit. Lucy had many admirable traits. Loyalty to her friends was one of them.

Mrs. Hackshaw had warned Sophie Gingembre that the children were not good candidates to pose for paintings since they lacked the ability to hold still. 'I have yet to meet a foundling who can refrain from moving, speaking, wriggling, scratching, or adjusting themselves for five minutes at a time, not to mind twenty-five.'

Mrs Hackshaw arranged the girls according to size, with Lucy at the back because she was the tallest. Sophie had other ideas. She moved Lucy to the front, placing little Polly to her right.

When Mrs Hackshaw protested, Sophie adopted a stern demeanour and spoke crossly.

'My dear Mrs Hackshaw. I'm sure that you are an excellent Matron and that you are an expert in everything that you do. However, I am an artiste. I am in the trained ancient tradition of drawing and painting the "human form divine" and this is the way I want things arranged.'

Mrs Hackshaw puffed herself up as though to reply, but before she could utter a word, the artist continued: 'I am searching for the inner radiance of the girls' human souls. Physical appearance is not important – fat or thin, short or tall, beautiful or plain, handsome or ugly, perfectly proportioned or not at all – it doesn't matter one whit!'

'But it's all back-to-front,' complained Sarah, now relegated to the back.

Sophie would brook no further complaints. The girls had to accept the order in which they were to position themselves.

Who could have thought, looking at the tranquil faces, the serene poses, that such turmoil lurked in the background? Studious Hetty was now to Lucy's left.

Jenny, also behind, had her mind on other things. Her new *objet d'amour*, seated in the boys' pew, was all that she could think about. The painting reflects her total indifference to what was happening all around her.

Sarah made good use of the knitting needle in her pocket to jab Lucy with it as often as she could, but nothing could break the spell for Lucy. Fascinated by the creative process, absorbed by the atmosphere of the hushed church, amazed by the concentration of the diligent artist, she vowed that one day, her talents would mark her out as someone special. She would become a famous artist in her own right.

The Audition

Mrs Carew looked at Lucy with great satisfaction. The teal-coloured dress, with its pretty ecru lace collar, showed off the girl's slim figure to best advantage.

'Nobody would take you for a maid in that dress,' the older woman exclaimed. 'Now, off you go, my dear. Chin up and show them what you can do.'

The twenty-minute journey to the Royal College of Music on Prince Consort Road passed in a blur of anxious jitters. Lucy's stomach was in a knot and when she nervously tested her voice, nothing came out except a helpless squawk. 'More like a seagull than a soprano,' she muttered hopelessly to herself.

At Notting Hill Gate, she turned left at the second cross street and, there, sure enough, was her destination on the right – a daunting, turreted, redbrick building, set in off the road. It was much grander than she had imagined.

Lucy made her way to the shiny, red door marked 'Entrance' and timidly tapped the brass knocker.

The woman who answered was dressed in a black skirt and white blouse with an opal cameo at the neck. Her hair was in a prim bun and Lucy estimated that she might be in her early forties. A badge on her blouse bore the name 'Miss A. Barker'.

'Good afternoon,' she barked. 'And you are...?'

Lucy tried not to giggle at how closely the lady's tone of voice resembled her name.

'I'm Lucy,' came the stammered reply.

'Oh yes, you're here to see Professor Montefiore. Come on in, then. He has a pupil with him now, but he won't be long.'

Lucy followed Miss Barker down a narrow hallway, black and white tiles laid hexagonally. She gaped at the grandeur of the wood panelling to elbow height and the flocked wallpaper to the ceiling.

Her escort opened a door on the right side of the corridor and led Lucy into what she announced was the anteroom.

'Take a seat there, Lucy,' she said. 'Mr Alexander is still with the professor, but he won't be much longer. Sit anywhere you like.'

Her abrupt departure gave Lucy an opportunity to look around. The waiting room was lined from floor to ceiling with bookshelves. Huge volumes – leather bound, green, red and dark blue books with gold lettering on the spines – filled the shelves. The display made her feel dizzy and she was glad to sit for a moment. She sank into a leather-bound armchair, like the one in Mr Peacock's study.

When her head cleared, she was able to tune into what was going on in the adjoining room – the music room, she surmised. The voices of two men carried clearly. An older voice suggested: 'Once again please, Mr Alexander, and then we'll finish'. A chord sounded on the piano and a young man began to sing.

Did you not hear my lady
Go down the garden singing?

Lucy was familiar with the piece, as it was popular at the Peacock's. But this young man expressed his wistful sadness in a way she had not heard before, almost to the point that she was surprised to hear the older voice cutting in. 'Thank you, Mr Alexander. We'll resume from there at the same time next week. Until then, please work hard on the vocal exercises we studied today.'

The music room door opened and a young man of about Lucy's age emerged. His tailored burgundy jacket and beige waistcoat emphasised his athletic form. His cravat matched his jacket and he carried that badge of the wealthy – a silver-topped cane.

He greeted Lucy jauntily on his way out. She inadvertently caught his eye as she returned his greeting. There was something in his frank, humorous gaze that was very appealing. But Lucy had no time to think about this. She was immediately and peremptorily summoned to the music room.

Lucy couldn't stop herself from shaking as she entered. She took her surroundings in at a glance – a good-sized room, sympathetically furnished. The upright piano was placed at an angle from the wall. The window behind the piano ensured that light was used to best advantage. The piano top was free from any bric-a-brac except for some sheet music. A standard lamp in bronze was placed at one side of the piano and in front of it was a chair with graceful spindles at the back, decorated with inlaid wood.

On the wall to the right, she spied a cabinet with doors. This was filled with more music, filed in orderly fashion away from the dust. The musical environment was completed with various plaster casts, bronzes, pictures and books. On the walls were rich hangings in subdued tints of green, complimented by the green velvet curtains.

All in all, a harmony of colours.

The professor at the piano stood to greet her. As he rose to his full height, Lucy observed a small man, dressed in black. The gold buttons on his waistcoat and a shiny watch chain lightened his sombre appearance. He looked over his monocle at Lucy and proclaimed: 'Good afternoon, young lady. I am Professor Montefiore.'

Lucy blushed.

'Pleased to meet you, Professor,' she mumbled.

'I understand you are a protégé of Professor Grove,' he continued. 'He asked me to meet with you.'

'I'm happy to be here,' said Lucy. 'I hope I'm not taking up too much of your time.'

'Nonsense, my dear,' said the Professor. 'Grove has a keen ear and I'm sure he wouldn't want to waste my time or yours. So, let's begin the audition.'

He returned to the piano and struck a chord with a flourish.

'Now, Lucy, we start with some vocal exercises to assess your tone and range. Please sing after me.'

He struck another chord.

'*Bella Signo-o-o-o-o-o-o-o-o-o-ora!*'

Lucy recognised the simple doh-mi-soh-doh that they had used to warm up in the Foundling Hospital choir practices. Though she had no idea what the words meant, she copied the sounds that she heard.

'Again, please,' said the Professor, striking another note. 'In a higher pitch this time.'

She sang again – *Bella Signora* – and he kept raising the pitch higher and higher until Lucy thought she could sing no more.

'Very good,' Professor Montefiore exclaimed. 'You have an excellent range, and you can easily sing a high C. Next, we'll need to learn about your musical skills. How is your sight-reading?'

'I don't know how to sight-read, sir', Lucy said.

'Well, can you clap the rhythm of this piece?' he asked, handing her a sheet of music.

Lucy might as well have been looking at Japanese for all the sense she could make from the black symbols.

'No, sir, I can't,' she mumbled.

Professor Montefiore stopped smiling and began drumming his fingers on the piano lid.

'Very well. Now, I'm going to play the C major scale. Can you sing the third note I play?'

By listening carefully and reproducing what she heard, Lucy managed to gloss over this test.

'That's fine, we'll move on. Can you tell me what these mean?'

He showed Lucy some musical symbols and markings – dynamics, accidentals, key signatures and clefs – which she would come to know well in later years. However, today, she was flummoxed. She was close to tears. Each 'I don't know' seemed to annoy the professor even further and it was all Lucy could do to stay in the room.

Finally, with a note of exasperation in his voice, Professor Montefiore plucked some sheet music from the top of the piano and almost shouted: 'Please sing what you see on this page'.

Lucy was in despair by now. Hadn't she said she couldn't read music? She knew she had wasted the professor's time and everybody else's too. She reached for her handkerchief, unable to control her tears and her rising sense of panic.

'Calm down, child, it's not the end of the world. I want you to take a couple of deep breaths and compose yourself. Then, look at the pages and see if you can make anything of them.'

Through her tears, Lucy did as she was told and picked up the music, expecting to be completely bested by the formidable task. Then, she read on the top of the page, *'Did you not hear my lady...',* and realised that it was the piece that Mr Alexander had been singing. She knew it! She could sing the piece without needing to read the music, or at least, she could try her very best.

She closed her eyes and imagined herself back in the Foundling Hospital chapel. How the soprano soloists had moved her! With new resolve, she poured her heart out.

Did you not hear my lady
Go down the garden singing?
Blackbird and thrush were silent
To hear the alleys ringing.

Professor Montefiore seemed taken aback, but, regaining his composure, began to accompany her on the piano. When they reached the end of the piece, he was the first to break the silence.

'You didn't read that, did you? You sang from memory?'

'Yes, sir, I know the piece well. It's often performed at the Peacock's musical evenings.'

After a sharp intake of breath, Professor Montefiore spoke again.

'Lucy, you have a beautiful voice. It's clear now why Professor Grove asked me to see you. He thinks you have great potential and I'm inclined to agree. But beautiful voices are ten a penny and you, my dear, are a half-baked product, a rough diamond. You know nothing of technique or theory. But you have a quality which I often struggle to instil in my pupils, and which sets you apart. You can give expression to what's behind the music. You're capable of being an actor as well as a singer. That's what's necessary for greatness.'

He stood up from the piano and walked with Lucy towards the door.

'Do you want to progress further, Lucy? Do you have what it takes to learn the theory and the techniques? Even learn new languages? Italian? Latin?'

Lucy's eyes widened in amazement.

'I'll be intrigued to see how far you can go, and I'm prepared to take you on myself. Please meet me at the same time next Thursday. We'll begin our journey together.'

A dumbstruck Lucy, forgetting her manners, ran for the door. Tears had welled up in her eyes and she could barely speak.

With her hand on the brass knob, she turned and whispered: 'Thank you, Professor, thank you, thank you.'

Then, she ran out the door.

Chance Encounters

Thursday could not come around quickly enough for Lucy. She had tossed and turned in her bed all week, sleeping fitfully. The passing days were scored through on her calendar. No matter how hard she tried to distract herself, her mind returned to Thursday.

Thursday.

The day of her next lesson.

When at last it arrived, she scanned her meagre wardrobe with dismay. *Oh! What am I to do? I can't wear that again! What about this? Oh no!* She burst into tears in her bedroom.

Mrs Carew heard the sobs as she was passing. *Had she been listening at the door all along?*

'Now, now, Lucy,' she spoke softly. 'No point in getting yourself into a state. There, there. Dry your eyes. Here. Use this.'

Mrs Carew produced a white hankie as if by magic. If she grimaced when Lucy deposited the entire contents of her nostrils loudly onto the delicate filigree lace, only the long mirror on Lucy's wardrobe noticed.

'Oh, Mrs Carew,' Lucy cried, 'I have nothing proper to wear. And my hair is a mess. I can't be seen to look like a servant when I go to Professor Montefiore.'

Mrs Carew arched an eyebrow.

'Begging your pardon, Mrs Carew. I didn't mean that you look like a....'

'That's quite enough, Lucy. Quite enough, indeed. Now you listen to me, young lady.'

Mrs Carew spoke. At times, her words were stern, but mainly her tone was calm and comforting. In no time at all, Lucy's breathing reverted to a normal rhythm, her shoulders relaxed, and she listened gratefully and peacefully to the words of the wiser, older woman.

'Mrs Carew,' she said, 'do you think I could have a little of your rouge?'

'My goodness, Lucy, that's an unusual request coming from you.'

'Yes,' Lucy stammered,' but if you remember last week, Mr Alexander believed I was a proper lady. I can't let myself down today.'

Mrs Carew helped her as best she could. 'Now look at that pretty, fresh face,' she exclaimed. 'I don't know why you want to go changing yourself for any young man – but I suppose I shouldn't forget. I was young once too.'

Lucy stepped out onto Westbourne Terrace to find herself in the middle of a deluge. Raindrops turned into hailstones as she pulled down her hood against the onslaught. They filled her shoes and battered against her face. The umbrella barely kept the rain off her sensible coat before turning inside out in the wind. By the time she arrived at her destination, panting with the effort, her shoes were soaking wet. She touched a finger to her face and confirmed that the rouge was coming down in streams. *Oh no! I must look like a clown!*

As she approached the Royal College, the door burst open and out tumbled a young man. To her horror she realised that it was none other than Mr Alexander.

There was no time for either of them to stop. The collision was as inevitable as it was disastrous. Lucy swayed towards the ground, but the young man managed to grab her and hold her upright. He was so embarrassed when he saw who he was holding but nowhere near as embarrassed as the rescued girl.

'I'm terribly sorry,' he stammered. 'I wasn't looking where I was... Are you all right? Oh, I'm so sorry... Miss, Miss?'

Lucy could barely catch her breath. She realised with a shock that it was not the collision that left her speechless. *I'm in his arms! He's holding me! Oh!*

Lucy's heart hammered and her knees weakened. She searched frantically for something to say. As she formulated the start of one sentence, it was immediately supplanted by the start of another. All she could do was gaze at her rescuer – *who also caused this to happen* – and smile a confused, bewildered grimace. *Why can't I think of anything to say?*

A glamorous young woman leaned her head out of the window of a waiting carriage.

'Lexie?' she called. 'What on earth are you up to? You'll destroy your jacket! Remember where we're going!'

Her voice rose with more than a trace of irritation. 'Come on, please! Now!'

Torn between trying to help Lucy and following the orders of the lady in the carriage, the young man hesitated. Even if he wished to run over to the carriage, what could he do with Lucy?

'Just a moment, Eva,' he shouted over his shoulder. Somehow, Lucy's arms had found their way around his neck. He leaned closer. *His breath on my face.* Unconsciously, Lucy's lips parted.

'I'm afraid I'm going to have to leave you here to rest on the step,' he whispered. He peeled Lucy's arms from around his neck. 'I do hope you will recover. I'm so sorry. It was entirely my fault. You see, I was rushing to ....'

'Lexie! Come here at once!'

The shrill voice left no room for dithering.

Lucy felt herself being dropped on the step and in an instant, her rescuer was moving towards the carriage. His long limbs got in his way as he scrambled aboard. It seemed as if he must leave one leg behind as the horses started up even before the carriage door closed.

They sped off in the direction of Kensington Gardens.

Lucy was on the verge of tears. *How pathetic I am! He's driving off with his glamorous lady friend and I'm here soaked to the skin. I wish I could disappear. Oh God! Make me disappear!*

Dejectedly, she rang the doorbell and waited for Mrs Barker to let her in.

'What on earth has happened to you, my dear?' the older lady said kindly.

Lucy stammered an explanation and, warding off her attentions, made her way down to the music room where Professor Montefiore was waiting for her.

The warm-up commenced with a sequence of trilling 'rrrrrrs', tongue-twisters and scales. Lucy could hardly muster the enthusiasm she needed and froze on the second arpeggio.

'What's got into you today?' demanded Montefiore.

'I'm sorry, Professor,' was all that Lucy could say.

'Sorry? Sorry? You arrive late, soaked to the skin, and now you can't raise your voice beyond a pathetic B flat? Don't you care at all, young lady?'

Lucy held her breath. She closed her eyes and wished she were far away.

Crossly, the professor resumed: 'Let's try this scale again. If you can't sing, you shouldn't be here.'

The professor re-played the scale on the piano. Lucy sang hesitantly at first. When she reached the top note, to her surprise, her voice held firm. For the next hour she concentrated on her singing and all thoughts about the disastrous start to her morning vanished from her mind.

As she was leaving, the professor walked her to the door. He gave her an umbrella.

'Borrow that, my dear,' he said gently, 'Try to avoid heavy rain showers. And remember that your voice is a precious gift, and you must always take care of it. Today, you have learned a valuable lesson.'

'A valuable lesson?' she replied, not sure what he was talking about.

'Yes, my dear... Mr Edison tells us that *'many of life's failures are people who did not realise how close to success they were when they gave up.'* Sing, Lucy, even when you don't feel like singing. Trust your voice will remain steadfast and true, even when you think it is going to let you down.'

On the long walk home, she ran over several scenarios in her head. Who was Lexie's companion? Lexie was obviously in love with her, but why had she so much power over him? Lucy determined her only option was to erase Lexie forever from her thoughts. There was nothing between them, despite what she had imagined, and there never could be.

Back in Westbourne Grove, she wearily changed her clothes. As usual, Mrs Carew was dying for news of the lesson, but Lucy was in no mood for chit-chat. Almost in tears again, she told her friend what had happened.

'I'll never be anyone,' she moaned.

'Nonsense!' her friend retorted. 'These people were born with silver spoons in their mouths, but they'll never match your talent.'

Mrs Carew left the bedroom. She stood on the landing for a minute or two. Then she returned to Lucy's door, opened it a fraction and whispered: 'You wait and see, Lucy. Your voice is your silver spoon. That's what will carry you through life.'

Lucy fell asleep with Mrs Carew's comforting words ringing in her ears.

Saturday was normally Lucy's day off, but today, she had agreed to do a special favour for Mrs Peacock. *It's the least I can do. She's incredibly kind about my singing lessons.* The

Peacocks were going to Ascot with a party of friends and were excited about the outing. As it was the governess' day off too, Lucy had agreed to entertain the children for the afternoon by taking them to the park for a picnic.

'Here you are, Lucy,' said Mrs Carew, handing her a wicker picnic basket. 'You've got cheese sandwiches in there for Miss Katie, banana sandwiches for Master George, and plenty of lemonade. Now, off you go and enjoy yourselves.'

They headed off on foot, Lucy carrying the basket, George bowling a hoop with a stick, and Katie tending to her doll as they walked.

In less than twenty minutes, they arrived at the entrance to Hyde Park. They ambled along for a while before settling near the Serpentine. On this fine day, the lake was crowded with boaters. From this vantage point they could see everything. Lucy spread a rug on the grass and the children devoured their picnic. George gulped back his lemonade and made burping noises, much to the disgust of his sister.

'Stop it, George,' she shrieked. 'You sound like a corner boy. I'll tell Mama that you belch like a sailor!'

'Tell-tale,' he retorted, as he belched some more.

Soon the band struck up, playing a series of popular marches. *The Washington Post*, *The Liberty Bell* and The *Stars and Stripes Forever* rang out one after another. Lucy closed her eyes and smiled. The sunny afternoon, the rousing music and the happy revellers invigorated her.

But her happiness was short-lived. Katie was stuffing the last of the cheese sandwiches into the doll's mouth when George took off at a lick, chasing his hoop down the slope towards the lake.

'Master George! Come back immediately,' Lucy screamed.

He ignored the shouts. George was on an adventure, and he wasn't about to stop for anyone. His hoop was Fandango, a wild stallion that he had trained to win the Ascot Gold Cup. But his horse was lazy and needed reminders to keep up the pace. George beat the hoop furiously and made it go faster and faster. His little legs were chasing the hoop at full pace when he ran out of road. The boy and the hoop clattered unceremoniously over the edge and into the lake!

Lucy caught hold of Katie and dragged her, half running, half walking, down the hill.

'Ouch,' shrieked Katie, 'that hurts!'

'George, George,' screamed Lucy, ignoring the pleas from his sister. 'Keep up, Katie! Oh God, George, George.'

Her worst fear was realised. A crowd had gathered at the place where George's hoop had rolled into the lake. It was bad luck that he fell in at a very deep spot. He was up to his neck in trouble. As Lucy drew nearer, she grew more and more alarmed. Still tugging the little girl, she saw George floundering and trying to keep his head above water.

He shouted: 'Miss Lucy! Miss Lucy! Help! Help!'

Lucy waded into the murky water.

'Stay there, Master George. Keep still!'

With great squelching steps she moved towards him, her long skirt bunching around her legs. All she was thinking about was saving the boy.

The mud was sticky. It began to suck her in.

A dawning realisation. *This is like quicksand. I can't move my legs.*

George was tantalisingly out of her reach. She made a huge lunge towards him.

'George, reach for my arm.'

'I can't! I can't!'

'Stay calm! I'll stretch out for you.'

From the corner of her eye, she saw a flash of white. A tall, young man had cast off his jacket and boots and waded out into the pond. His white shirt changed to muddy brown in an instant.

He grabbed the boy roughly by the hair, saying in a strong voice:

'I'm going to turn you around on your back. You must not resist me.'

With a graceful movement, he flipped and floated George with his right hand while catching Lucy with his left. His arm around her waist, he half-lifted her and hoisted her towards the shore. The floating boy was like a rag doll in his wake. Without ceremony, he landed the two of them onto the grass verge.

'Look at my catch!' he exclaimed to all and sundry. 'A large salmon and a small trout!'

George was spitting out muddy water. Katie came to hold his hand.

'Keep spitting, young trout,' shouted the rescuer. 'You've swallowed half the Serpentine, young 'un. Better out than in!'

He turned his attention to Lucy who was gasping for breath. Now that she saw him clearly, she recognised him. It was Harry, the butcher-boy, who made the weekly meat deliveries to the Peacock household.

'Well, Lady Salmon! Decided to go for an early bath, didya? Next time, take yer clothes off first!'

He doubled up with laughter at his own joke.

Shaken and sobbing, Lucy was indignant.

'I beg your pardon,' she blurted.

'*I beg your pardon,*' he imitated her. 'First time a salmon has begged pardon from me?'

Lucy started to cry.

'Oh there, there, missy,' Harry said. 'No need for that. Just having some fun. You're a sorry sight, to be sure. Let's move you up into the sun to dry out.'

The only clean one among them was Katie. George's face was streaked with mud and tears. Lucy's once-white blouse was destroyed, her black skirt and boots ruined. The young man, who seemed none the worse for wear, was determined to turn the entire episode into an hilarious adventure. And, in truth, the more they talked about it, the funnier it seemed.

'The look on your face,' Harry laughed.

'How do you think I felt?' Lucy said. 'George and I were being sucked under.'

'I was all right,' said George. 'I was just splashing around and then Harry pulled me by the hair.'

Katie joined in: 'If it wasn't for Harry, you mightn't be so brave now!'

Lucy brought the analysis to a close.

'We are all thankful to Harry. He saved us from a serious incident. Let's just forget about it now and enjoy the park.'

By the time everyone had dried out, Lucy, Harry, George, and Katie were firm friends. Lucy studied the young man – tall and well built, a humorous face, rather pale. *Strong arms.* He entertained the children with a stream of genial nonsense. She watched them hooting with laughter as he came out with joke after joke, each sillier than the last.

The other day when it was so cold, a friend of mine went to buy some long underwear.

The shopkeeper said to him, 'How long do you want it?'

And my friend said,

'Well, from about September to March.'

'More! More!' shrieked the children.

I know a man with a wooden leg named Smith.

Oh really? What's the name of his other leg?

Time was moving on and Lucy had to bring the fun to a halt.

'Well, I suppose we ought to be getting back,' she said, standing up to leave. 'It's been lovely meeting you, Harry.'

'My pleasure, Miss Lucy, to be sure.' He exaggerated a mocking bow.

Mary Rose Tobin

'Thank you once again for your kindness,' Lucy said, as she shunted the two children along in front of her.

'Oi,' Harry called out. 'I was wondering if I might walk you all home.'

'Yes! Yes! Hooray for Harry!' clamoured the children.

'Well, I suppose so,' said Lucy. 'The Peacocks won't be back for another while, but we all need to get changed before they see us like this.'

'You live with peacocks, then?'

'No, silly!' said Katie. 'We are the Peacocks!'

They laughed and laughed at the silliness of it all.

Harry had the last word.

'Peacock, salmon and trout,
Swimming in the muddy slime
"Oh, help us, please get us out!"
Harry saved them from the Serpentine!'

He sang, and soon they were all chorusing the silly rhyme.

The little party gathered themselves and prepared to walk back to Westbourne Grove.

The crowds in the park had dispersed. The quiet path was dappled by the late afternoon sun. Lucy felt better. *Thank goodness nobody will see us looking like ragamuffins. Another twenty minutes and everything will be back to normal.*

Harry was chasing the children and they were screaming in mock terror. Then, Lucy heard him say: 'Good afternoon, Mr Alexander, Miss Eva.'

And there in front of them, taking the afternoon air, was Lucy's fellow student from the Royal College. He was walking towards them, accompanied by the lady Lucy had seen with him in the carriage on Thursday.

Miss Eva's dress was a deep green, with puffed sleeves and a black trim at the neck, bodice, and hem. She carried a matching parasol. Her long chestnut hair was arranged in ringlets. She couldn't have looked more different to the scruffy party in front of her.

'Well, hello, Harry,' Mr Alexander replied. 'Is this your...?'

He stopped abruptly when he saw Lucy bringing up the rear of the little procession.

'Surely that's not...? But it is! Miss Lucy! You're soaked through every time I see you! I didn't know you and Harry...?'

Lucy's mortification was complete. Mr Alexander could be in no doubt now that she was not who she pretended to be. And for him to see her in this state! She blushed so red she thought she would surely combust.

The awkward silence that ensued was broken by the sharp tones of Mr Alexander's companion.

'Come along, Lexie! Stop dilly-dallying. You know we're in a hurry to get there!'

And with a swing of her parasol, she brought the chance encounter to an abrupt end.

Love, Friendship, Revenge, and Growth

Les Amants d'un Jour
(with a nod to Edith Piaf)

It's another day at work. Here I am, my dreams of university long passed. That disastrous spell at the Sorbonne, full of fear and trepidation, waiting for someone to uncover me for the fraud I really was. My Master's degree – an unqualified success. And Florian – one more catastrophe in a long series of failed relationships. 'Another suitcase in another hall,' I hum, as I dry the glasses.

When I was a student, I passed this bar at least once a week. I peered through the window a million times without ever quite making it through the door, despite desperately wanting to. Back then I was a wispy Paris bohemian, with holes in my soles, reading about zinc bars in the library's copy of Émile Zola's *The Belly of Paris*. But to my student eyes the patrons looked too frightening, the proprietor too crotchety, the cigarette smoke too thick and the housekeeping too skimpy for me ever to venture in there.

Things change. Now I work here every day, up to my elbows in soapy water, drying glasses and inhaling the cigarette fumes and other stale aromas which fill the dusty air. In the mornings, before the bar opens, I clean out the few *chambres à louer* which make up the second floor of the building – bare walls, thin carpets and a million stories to tell.

The bar is freestanding; horseshoe shaped and made of the obligatory zinc. There are pulley lights, with doily-draped shades, and makeshift cubbyholes for stacking wine bottles. The walls are grimy and yellowed, with crocheted curtains hanging on the smoky windows.

Blackboards announcing the *plats du jour* hang behind the bar and the tables are covered with paper tablecloths over red-and-white checked cotton ones. Wine is served in unbreakable Duralex tumblers of varying sizes.

Regulars treat this place like home, coming and going, reading and gossiping, daydreaming and grumbling. The air hums with soccer chat. Early evening, the crowd becomes more mixed – young couples with babies, the local drunks, and the after-work imbibers.

It's not quite the worst job I ever had, but it gets close. And each week I save a little, to get me back home and put this nightmarish episode of my life behind me.

It was an ordinary Monday afternoon. I looked up from drying the glasses to see a young couple lingering shyly at the bar, slight waifish figures silhouetted in the shaft of sunlight streaming in from the open door. They had an aura about them which made my heart stop for a moment... or maybe I just think that now....

'Can I help you?'

'We'd like a room until tomorrow.'

Well, this was an ordinary enough request, we dealt with furtive young lovers every day... but there was something different about these two.

I showed them up to the bare little room, tucked away in the dark shadows, all the while noticing that they seemed to carry the sunshine with them, illuminating the shabby setting with an almost ethereal glow.

Les Amants d'un Jour

Closing the door on them, I sank back down the stairs to resume my station behind the bar.

What do I care about them anyway? Lovers come and go here, just as they do in my own life.

Why did it have to be me who found them next day? Still holding hands, still face to face, but all the sunshine drained from them along with their lives.

Despite their apparent youth they had planned well and were quite without identification or possessions. Nobody claimed them as they lay cold in the anonymous Paris morgue.

Of course, I had no connection to them. But I was there when they were laid to rest in the sunshine. And as the sad little ceremony ended, my mind wandered to the ribbon she wore and the look on his face.

Why do I let this hurt me? I must stop thinking about them. I have to earn money and save to get out of here....

My eye catches the *chambres á louer* sign.

CRASH...

Another indestructible Duralex glass falls loudly to the floor and shatters in a million pieces.

'*Merde,*' I say, in my best French.

Seville Oranges

There is a moment when one teeters on the brink of falling in love, a delicious tension between pulling back and taking the plunge. I had reached that point. The stereotypical pattern of casual interest at first, leading to fascination, to flirtation, to infatuation, and finally, to love, did not apply in this case. For me, Heather was a drug so potent that our first meeting immediately led to addiction. I plunged straight to infatuation and was considering taking the leap of faith that constitutes love.

My waking thoughts were consumed by her and she populated my dreams. Perhaps the taboo against same sex relationships, neither fashionable nor legal in the Catholic Ireland of the 1980s, helped to heighten the intensity of my feelings. There is no stronger aphrodisiac than an illicit love affair.

But the truth is there was nothing to it. These romantic notions were all in my mind. I really did not know how Heather felt. We never even kissed, except in that sisterly, friendly way that involves an embrace and a peck on the cheek. No. This 'love affair' was undramatic. It never received a public airing. It was all imaginary.

Heather may have sensed something. Maybe she felt that our relationship, such as it was, was a bit too intense, too personal. Maybe she was not ready for a commitment. She may have had no attraction towards women. Whatever the reason, the way I was cut off and isolated from her was brutal and hurtful. Not knowing the reasons why was worse than the sense of rejection. I carried this scar for most of my adult life.

So, when I received the call from Cassie, Heather's sister, to say that Heather was anxious to meet with me, my heart leapt.

'Of course, of course,' I babbled, scrabbling to find a pen to write down the address. 'I'll be there tomorrow at eleven.'

Details were scant, but I gathered that time was not our ally. I was determined to repair our friendship for whatever span remained. We would talk, and, finally, I would come to understand what had gone wrong all those years ago.

I was twenty-five years old when I first met Heather. It was my first posting away from home. I was working in a regional hospital in the west of Ireland. My father had somehow arranged accommodation for me, through the nod-and-wink system, with a relative of a local politician. Whatever strings were pulled or whatever wheels were greased, I ended up renting an entire three-bedroomed house on the Main Street, which I had all to myself.

One evening, as I was having tea in the hospital canteen, a strange woman appeared at the doorway. I could not help staring at her. With her tall frame, blonde hair and colourful bohemian dress, she was an unusual sight in this staid setting. She ordered coffee, and to my surprise, after a quick word with the server, she headed directly over to my table.

'Hello! I'm Heather,' she said. 'I came to find you because I heard that you might be looking for a lodger.'

The thought had not, in fact, occurred to me, but it suddenly seemed like a good idea.

'I'm not here much,' she went on, 'only when the courts are sitting, or to see a client on probation. But I'm fed up staying in the hotel.'

'Yes, okay, I have a bedroom you can use. And a little sitting room too,' I heard myself saying.

I remember very little of the subsequent conversation, so engrossed was I in absorbing every detail of this fascinating woman. The way her lips moved; how she tossed back her hair; how she curled her fingers in a ball to emphasise a point – everything about her was just riveting.

The following evening, she moved in. As I helped Heather unpack and settle, I was intrigued by her personal items – her clothes, her travel cases, her make-up, and perfume, her general paraphernalia, were all a source of wonder. I began to look forward to her monthly visits.

Heather was a social worker with the courts. She was of indeterminate age – probably ten years my senior – and she seemed to know everyone and everything. She adopted a 'big sister' attitude towards me and considered it her duty to introduce me to every aspect of country living – ploughing championships, race meetings, county shows, high teas, summer festivals, sherry receptions, Barbour jackets – these were all new to me and I embraced them enthusiastically.

When the courts were sitting in Sligo, Heather lodged on the Ashbury Estate, in an old farm cottage surrounded by acres of woodland, gardens and grounds. I was thrilled to be invited there for weekends, to join in parties and excursions with her many friends. To this day I don't know how she got these lodgings – it would not even surprise me if she tackled Sir Alfie Ashbury as he took tea in the House of Lords. She had a key to the main house, a cut stone, three-storey building with a classical Georgian façade. One day, we went to the house, reaching it by walking along a magnificent avenue of ancient limes, which met high overhead to form a continuous arch of foliage. Birdsong, bluebells, wild garlic – she identified and explained everything.

'How did you get the key?' I asked nervously.

'Never mind that, we're going to see something amazing,' she said. 'Lord Ashbury keeps his Paul Henrys under the beds.'

For all I knew, Paul Henry could have been a dance in a Jane Austen novel, or a range of fashion items, but I was happy to go along for the adventure. Sure enough, once inside the semi-abandoned house, she began to haul large, dusty paintings from under the beds, saying with all the assurance of a Christie's auctioneer, 'Look, here, this is a Paul Henry, and this one? Would you believe it? A Jack Yeats. And over here? Mildred Anne Butler.'

If I knew then what I know now, I doubt I'd have left empty handed.

It was in the little farm cottage that Heather allowed herself to relax fully. She seemed at one with her environment and she knew instinctively what needed to be done. I fell into a pattern of visiting her at weekends. Arriving late on a Friday evening, having travelled the bumpy roads over bogland and mountainous terrain, I was often cold, tired and hungry. The last thing I wanted to do was to keep house. But, once Heather got home, she leaped into action. In no time at all, the fire was roaring, a delicious meal, made from what she called 'emergency rations', was bubbling on the stove and the vases were filled with twigs, grasses and wild flowers gathered in an instant from outside. Lined with books, lit by candlelight and the glow from the log fire, the shabby furniture disguised with casually thrown Foxford rugs, the cottage was a haven.

The last time I stayed, Heather was throwing a huge Valentine's party. Catering and entertaining were her forte and I remember how she fed the large gathering with boeuf Bourguignon, baked potatoes, tossed salads and cream-laden desserts. The wine flowed freely, and the assembled guests – Heather's special friends – were worldly wise, arty, and enthralling. The fact that they were all that bit older than me made them seem more sophisticated and cosmopolitan. I revelled in the experience.

Waking up next morning, somewhat the worse for wear, I saw bodies everywhere. Nobody ever went home after Heather's parties. Big breakfasts, and long walks on the nearby beaches or cliffs, cleared our heads in preparation for the journey back and the week's work ahead.

These were blissful times but inevitably, things had to change. My promotion and transfer to Dublin happened suddenly, and shortly afterwards, Heather was moved to a new circuit on the east coast.

For a while, it looked as if our lifestyle could reinvent itself, albeit on a different coastline. Heather quickly found another country cottage; she had a new entourage of friends and, in no time at all, it seemed like she had lived there forever. We continued to see a lot of each other. Both voracious readers, we swapped books and gossip. She found interesting plays and other events for us to go to, and she always knew – or at least knew about – the people we came across in the course of our adventures. Whether she was dissecting a play, or filleting an acquaintance, she was the best of company.

I was about to celebrate my thirtieth birthday. Heather had such plans. It was going to be the biggest and best bash ever. She had already started baking cakes. Yes. Cakes.

'Tiers,' she said. 'A cake as big as the Empire State Building. Only the best for my best friend. My only true friend.'

These words caused my heart to leap.

News of the botched operation to solve a recurring sinus problem came to me in a garbled phone message from a nurse I knew in the Eye and Ear Hospital.

'Your friend, Heather, she's out of theatre. She's been asking for you. Do you think you might be able to get over here?'

I cycled as fast as I could, down along by the canal, across Leeson St Bridge to Adelaide Road, and almost tripped running up the steps to the hospital. At the nurses' station, they assured me that her operation had gone well and that she would soon be transferred to the Recovery Ward. The sight of her poor bruised and bandaged face, with swollen eyes, shocked me.

She seemed confident that all would be well. Then, she developed a persistent nasal drip, which turned out to be leaking cerebrospinal fluid, necessitating a further operation. How I wept the night I visited her in Beaumont after her brain surgery.

Once she was well enough to travel, I planned a holiday for us to Dingle, a place I was very much looking forward to seeing. I was also eagerly anticipating having Heather all to myself for a week. It turned into the holiday from hell.

The surgeons had explained that in order for them to operate, Heather's brain had to be lifted from her skull. The consequence, they said, for some patients could be a change in personality. Even though I was aware of this, I found Heather's moods, crankiness and constant irritability almost impossible to deal with, and I spent most of the holiday in Dingle wishing it was over.

From then on, our friendship took a downturn. Heather became judgmental and had something hurtful to say about everything – my friends, my spending habits, my taste in clothes, and my career choices. To my enduring sadness, we stopped seeing each other as often, and then hardly at all. I could not understand how our perfect friendship could turn so sour, so quickly.

It is hardly surprising now, looking back, that she became angry and depressed. Her cancer diagnosis was the last straw. Visiting her in hospital the first night she was admitted for tests – before she knew – I brought wine, food, gossip magazines and candles. We created a party atmosphere in the grim ward, much to the disgust of the elderly nun in the other bed.

There wasn't much more fun after that.

As her illness progressed, I did my best to spend time with her, until, eventually, she forbade it. 'You're too bubbly,' she said. 'I don't want to see you anymore.'

After she got out from hospital, it became too difficult for her to live alone in her cottage. Eventually, she moved in with her sister. I kept in touch with Cassie by phone and I knew that things weren't looking good.

Then came the day of the phone call and my journey to Cassie's home in the midlands. When I arrived, Cassie led me into a downstairs bedroom, having warned me of the effects of the morphine. Heather was propped up in what looked like a hospital bed, her eyes shining. I could see that her thoughts were racing.

'I've written a letter for you,' she said. 'It explains everything. Read it and you'll understand. Here, open it.'

I took the letter but hesitated before opening it. I felt that it must contain the solution to the terrible puzzle of our damaged relationship. She would tell me that I was forgiven, that I was her love after all. I knew I couldn't read such an emotional letter without breaking down. I felt tears welling at the back of my eyes as I replied: 'Heather, I'd rather talk to you now and read the letter later. Just tell me how you are.'

'Okay,' she said, 'but don't forget it when you leave; it's terribly important.'

For the next hour or so, she spoke deliriously, a stream of consciousness, a cascade of impossible fantasies, airy fairy ideas and dream-like ambitions. Without stopping for breath, she told me about her plans to develop a place of pilgrimage at the wishing well on her home farm. It was, she said, renowned by its association with a saint.

'I'm preparing a guest list. I want everyone there on the Feast Day in October. You must come.'

She elaborated on the catering plan, wildly arranging evening entertainment and accommodation for the guests. I found the conversation exhausting, but she was animated. This was not how I wanted things to go. We had more important matters to talk about.

But I did not interrupt, confident I would find my answers in the letter. Her conversation tailed off and soon she slept. I called Cassie to let her know I was going.

With the letter safely tucked into my handbag, I made my farewells and headed for the car. My emotions were in turmoil. My head was reeling, and my stomach churned with a mixture of terrible sadness, anxiety and anticipation. The letter would explain all, I was sure of that.

I needed a quiet comfortable place to draw breath before facing its contents. Looking everywhere along the road for somewhere suitable, I noticed a petrol station with tables outside and a sign advertising coffees and teas. Pulling in, I bought a take-away Americano and settled myself at one of the wooden picnic benches. The day was still bright, and a watery sunlight trickled onto the table. I slowly opened the envelope, and this is what I read:

My dear friend,

Thank you for coming to see me today.
On your way home, when you are approaching Kildonan, go into the village. It's huge now, but a village just the same.
There's a butcher there, I think Fallons or Falveys, opposite the supermarket. They sell everything, it's very upmarket.
Lovely marinades, deli beef and ham, home-made sausages with herbs and such, very cheap, not much meat in them. T-bone steaks, even venison. And lamb shanks.
Lots of helpful staff, and in season they sell a sort of home-made marmalade made from Seville oranges. I hope it's not all gone now.
So just make sure you buy the Seville orange marmalade.
See you.
Best wishes,

Heather

Hijacked

Julie was a schoolteacher for forty years, a principal for twenty of those. Now that she had retired, the decision to go back to college to study History of Art was the best one she had ever made. In her insulated world as a school principal, the only things that mattered were timetables, meetings and more timetables. When school holidays came – extended with a few course days thrown in – the cottage in Connemara was her escape. That was how her years were punctuated.

Art had become her new passion. A creative world of beauty and culture had opened up to her and she embraced it wholeheartedly. More diligent than her younger classmates, she was usually to be found in the library with her head in some magnificently illustrated book or other.

On this particular day, she was indulging in a little nostalgia. Moments from her teaching life rose to the surface, then disappeared again. St Declan's School was in a notorious area of the city. Unemployment was rife, most of the parents didn't work and the children she taught seemed sure to face the same future. She remembered how, in her early years of teaching, the twelve-year-old First Years enrolled in September, all shiny faced and innocent. Things had changed in recent times. An air of cynicism had crept in, even with the younger children, who were already out of control. Maintaining discipline was the hardest part of a teacher's job. Teaching the children to read, a skill that they often didn't master in primary school, came after law and order had been established.

She wondered if she had ever made a difference. All those long, hard days, all those sleepless nights, all that worrying. Maybe, at most, she consoled herself, she had made things better for one or two children.

An image of a girl with sad eyes and shining dark hair came floating into her mind. Rhianna. Yes, Rhianna was her name. She had 'soul'. She had arrived in school unable to read two words. In after-school tutoring, Julie had made great strides with her; first teaching her the fundamentals of basic English, and then, instilling in her an enjoyment of the written word. Together they read: *The Diary of a Junkie*; *The Secret Diary of Adrian Mole aged 13¾*; and *The Diary of Anne Frank*.

Rhianna was persuaded to keep a diary of her own. Sometimes they read extracts from the diary together, and Julie caught a glimpse of the reality of home life for this child. Rhianna remarked, one day, that Anne Frank's situation was better than her own.

Julie stirred from her poignant reverie. The library was growing quiet, and many of the students had packed their books and headed off – most of them to the pub, she speculated.

No pub for Julie.

Tonight, she was going to the last choir practice before the upcoming Spring concert. She beeped her car open and left the university, the evening closing in around her.

Pulling up outside the Band Hall where the choir rehearsed, she loosened her seatbelt. As she did, there was a tap on the passenger window. She turned reflexively, expecting to see one of her choir friends. But then she heard the rear door opening and with a rising sense of panic, she realised that someone had got into the car.

No! More than one person.

Her glance moved from the passenger window to the back seat where two young men stared brazenly at her. They were indistinguishable from one another by the uniform of hoodies they wore.

Instinctively, she clicked the car into parking gear, removed the keys from the ignition and got out.

Displaying a bravado she certainly didn't feel, she marched around the car to the passenger side where the third hooded figure stood. She was about to launch into a headmistress's lecture about respecting the rights and property of others, when she caught a glimpse of a familiar face, peeping from under the hood.

'Rhianna! How are you keeping? I haven't seen you in ages. How's Granny getting on? It's nearly time for me to go and visit her again. She always has lovely chocolate biscuits with the tea.'

Julie would have carried on, talking in pleasantries, had she not been interrupted.

'I'm sorry, Miss.'

This from Rhianna in a thin voice, almost a whisper.

'Sorry, Rhianna?' said Julie. 'Sure, there's nothing to be sorry for at all. Isn't it great that we met up like this?'

The girl shifted uncomfortably from foot to foot.

Looking towards the back seat, Julie continued: 'And your two friends were right to get in out of the wind. It's a cold night.'

'Thank you, Miss.'

Those same sad eyes.

'Don't mention it, dear. It's so nice to see you. Really, it is. Let me know a good time to visit Granny?'

'I will, Miss.'

Turning to her two companions, Rhianna shouted at them: 'Hey, youse! Have ye nothin' better to do than warming your arses, sorry Miss, in Miss O'Grady's car? Get out and let's go.'

The two boys elbowed each other. One of them shouted back:

'Wha'?'

'Get out! *Now*,' Rhianna growled through gritted teeth.

Still jostling, the two boys crawled out, hid their heads deeper in their hoodies, and ran away.

Rhianna held back.

Julie, who was now shaking, was unsure whether to be grateful or angry. She mumbled a few words of thanks.

Rhianna placed a hand on the older woman's shoulder and looked her straight in the eye.

'You had my back once,' she sniffed.

Before Julie could reply, the girl turned and ran off, melting into the shadows.

Best Served Cold

Jill knew there was something wrong the minute the principal made a beeline in their direction.

'Good morning, Billy,' Mr Flaherty called out breezily. Billy stood stock still beside his mother with his mouth agape. He clutched his schoolbag in front of his chest, a shield against threat. Jill ran her hands through her messy brown curls and zipped up her rain jacket to hide the old jeans and t-shirt she had pulled on that morning. She had a sinking feeling that the two of them – mother and son – were about to be pitted against the world once more.

'Run along to your class now,' the principal said, 'I want a quick word with your mother.' Billy glanced up at her. She nodded and mouthed the word, 'Go!' She watched as he slouched away, still clasping his bag with both hands.

'Mr Flaherty,' she said, turning her attention to the diminutive figure, whose little legs had carried him across the schoolyard with great urgency to confront her. Some of the other mothers had gathered to observe, curious to pick up a bit of gossip.

'Mrs Sullivan,' the principal began, 'we need to talk about Billy.'

'If it's about his schoolwork, Mr Flaherty, I can tell you that he does his homework first thing. And I check it for him.'

Jill stood, hands on hips, with a come-one, come-all, but-you-won't-best-me attitude. Mr Flaherty hesitated. She was a foot taller than him, enabling her to look down and see where his thinning hair was yielding to an oval bald spot. His efforts at keeping his scalp covered were useless in the wind. He had small hands, and his tiny fingers kept trying to fix the loose strands in place. She imagined him as an army soldier saluting her. Major Comb-Over.

'No, no,' he stammered, 'your son's academic work is fine.'

'What is it, then?'

By now, a larger gaggle of mothers had convened close by, the better to catch the conversation. Any morsel of gossip was treasured, especially if it involved the Sullivans. Hadn't their marriage provided the whole town with a spectacle that kept the chattering classes busy for weeks? The Monday morning gym workouts had become dull since William had set up home in Lorraine's apartment. There was little interest in the wife left behind with the young son. All eyes were on the glamorous couple and the direction that their relationship would take. But rumour had it that all was not sweetness and light in Paradise. William's roving eye was a source of much debate.

'Billy had no gym clothes again last week,' said the principal, feeling more confident now that he had imparted the message. In a voice loud enough for his audience to hear he asked: 'Can you remind him to bring them this week?'

Jill wished that she could tell this trumped-up little officer to be more discrete. Business of this nature should be conducted in the privacy of his office. Her face reddened and she fought back the impulse to shout. Instead, she murmured: 'I'll make sure he won't forget.'

With one hand grasping at his flying strands of hair, Mr Flaherty was about to say something else, but Jill turned on her heel. She glared at the women gathered near the exit and rushed out the gate. In the safety of her car, she let the tears flow. As if I haven't enough trouble. Billy has outgrown his kit. Where will I get the money?

She drove the short distance to the charity shop.

The familiar smells of old clothes, sweat and air freshener greeted her as she swung the door open. The shop looked festive; the abundant Christmas decorations certainly cheered the place up. But there was no disguising the shabbiness of the men's and women's clothing hanging on the racks in the centre of the floor. Compared with the Christmas TV ads, the toys and children's books along the back wall looked sad and tired. The scarves and jewellery along the side section were tatty, the mismatched dishes, plates, jugs, and mugs unappealing. The only decent selection was in the array of bookshelves, lined with new and nearly new volumes in every genre. Something for everyone there, Jill often thought.

Hannah, the manager, was at the till. She wore that incongruous Indian cotton dress, its vivid peacock colours proclaiming to the world that she was a child of the sixties. Her beads jingled as she looked up to greet her colleague.

'Morning, Jill.'

'Morning, Hannah. Sorry I'm late.'

Hannah noticed the shake in Jill's voice. She scrutinised the tear-stained face. She knew instinctively that Jill's veneer of insouciance was about to crumble.

'What is it, love?' Hannah asked.

Jill was always tough when the odds were against her. She could fight for herself and her son with fierce determination. She could cope with sternness and aggression. But the first sign of kindness slayed her. She started to sob.

'Oh, come on, loveen.' Hannah's bangles jangled as she put a hand on Jill's shoulder. 'We'll have a cuppa, and you can tell me what's happened. No customers at this hour – they won't even be able to find the shop with that mess outside.'

The supermarket next door had erected scaffolding last week. Nobody bothered to tell Hannah about the plans for a major renovation and facelift. People could barely see the front of the charity shop with all the workers and cherry pickers and canvas sheets flapping incessantly in the wind. The footfall in the shop had decreased noticeably since all of this began.

The two women moved into the galley kitchen which served as a staffroom. You could tell that everything in the kitchen had been salvaged from donations. Jill selected some mugs from among the array hanging on hooks over the counter. She rummaged in the cupboard and fished out a sugar bowl and an opened packet of digestives, before sinking into one of the canvas director's chairs.

Hannah lit a cigarette and offered one to Jill. 'I quit, remember?' said Jill as she took the proffered offering. When she had lit up, taken a deep drag to the bottom of her lungs and exhaled a plume of smoke, she felt better. Over the noise of the kettle, she told Hannah about the school, and Billy. 'And it's not only the gym clothes. Where will I get his art materials? How can I face the endless bills?'

'You know, it's a year today since he walked out,' she wept. 'And he's never given me one cent since. The court date isn't until the end of January, and I still haven't paid back the loan for the schoolbooks, never mind getting Billy anything for Christmas.'

Hannah pushed a box of tissues across the table.

'And Lorraine, of all people! Supposed to be my best friend!' Jill cried harder. She dabbed her eyes and blew her nose. A slideshow of images played in her mind. Lorraine and herself at the Debs ball. The Leaving Cert holiday in Ibiza. The fun they had in college. Lorraine at her wedding. The beautiful bridesmaid, all over the dashing groom... William the Conqueror.

The older woman listened attentively as Jill spoke, nodding now and then, shushing tenderly whenever Jill broke down, giving her time and space to release all her suppressed heartache.

'I know you don't want sympathy,' she said after a while. 'But charity begins at home. If you see anything in the shop that might help with Billy, or Christmas, take it with you. After all, we're here to assist people in need. Just because you work here doesn't mean that you can't avail of our help. I won't ask any questions. You're a good worker, and you deserve any break you can get.'

Jill smiled gratefully and got up to rinse the mugs. 'Will we get started then?'

'I think you should work in the back room today,' Hannah said. 'Maybe do the till after lunch. Have a quiet morning. Do you good.'

Feeling better, Jill opened the door to the back room. Her eyes were met by a jumble of bags, boxes, and containers of all descriptions. An iron and ironing board were set up in the middle of the floor, adjacent to a laundry steamer. Down one side were the two long trestle tables where staff and volunteers sat and worked.

The donated bags contained everything you could possibly imagine. You never knew what the next contribution would bring. Jill thought of it as the detritus of other people's lives.

To an outsider the room might have seemed totally chaotic, but by now Jill was used to the work of sorting through the bags and pricing the items. She had learned many skills since she started to work in the shop in September. She could tell if items were designer or fake. She knew how to identify crystal from cheaper glass.

Hannah was a knowledgeable mentor. 'Real leather is flexible and soft to the touch,' she told her. 'But it also has a grainy feel.' Hannah held up two pieces of leather. 'Smell the difference,' she said to Jill. Very quickly Jill learned that genuine leather has a distinct, oaky smell, whereas faux leather does not.

In the early days Jill spent a couple of hours in the library, where the librarian explained the Dewey System of cataloguing books. In no time at all, she became adept at sorting the dozens of books that were donated every day.

Pricing wasn't too difficult – jackets were €4, shirts or blouses €3, and t-shirts could be bought for a euro.

She sat behind the first trestle table and started to sort through the nearest black bag. A bit calmer now, she worked on autopilot, lost in thought. After a while she got up to switch the radio from the blaring *Christmas FM* to something quieter – *Lyric* would do. Nearing the door, she heard some activity going on outside and paused to listen.

Hannah was talking to a woman who had obviously brought in a donation. Jill could hear snatches of the conversation: 'My husband is being posted abroad, and we're moving soon. We can't possibly take all this stuff with us.' She could hear Hannah helping the donor to bring in the bags.

When the woman had gone, Jill offered to assist Hannah. Together they heaved four huge black sacks onto a trolley. Then they moved them easily to the back store.

Hannah went back to the till.

Full of curiosity, Jill began to investigate the new donation. The first bag she opened contained shirts and she tipped them out on the ground. Preparing to price them she saw that some were new, tags still on.

Ralph Lauren, TM Lewin, Marks and Spencer. This is good stuff, no Dunnes or Penney's here...

Intrigued, she moved onto the second bag. This one was full of sportswear, most of which seemed new. Nike, Adidas – all the big labels.

She tipped out the contents of the third bag, which was full of sweaters, in similar condition to the previous contents. By now a nagging thought was bothering her – somehow, some of the items were vaguely familiar. But it was only when she picked up the green monogrammed sweater, with 'WS' in entwined gold letters, that she realised what she was dealing with.

The fourth bag contained suits and work jackets. Frantically scrabbling through the contents, she came upon another item she recognised – a handmade silk suit with no label.

The bastard! We got that made on our holiday in Vietnam!

Her brain fizzed as she tried to make sense of the situation. What on earth is going on? Why am I sorting through four bags of my exe's clothing? Lorraine? Was it Lorraine I heard earlier talking with Hannah?

Sorting and pricing the contents of the four sacks took Jill up to lunchtime. She went for a walk to clear her head and returned to assume her position at the till. The shop wasn't busy - until a few youths in school uniforms barged in. They started to roam around the shop, picking up and dropping items, laughing and messing. School's out! Better watch these kids! Jill's supervision was interrupted by the sharp trill of her mobile phone. She fished it out of her pocket and looked at the screen. Emer. Her sister.

'Jill, Jill, I have news!'

'What is it? What's going on?'

'I'm just out of the gym. I heard a conversation you'd be interested in.'

'Now, Emer, you know I don't have time to ...'

'You'll have time for this!'

'What?'

'She's thrown him out!'

'What? Who?'

'Lorraine and William. She's after throwing him out!'

Jill felt faint.

'Are you sure?'

'Yeah, he wasn't coming home in the evenings. Up to his old tricks. They had a huge row, and she gave him his marching orders, said she wasn't having him living like a lord in her apartment. He could go to hell and fend for himself!'

Jill was at a loss for words.

'Emer, this solves a big mystery for me – no, I'll tell you later. I can't talk now, I'm at the till.'

'Okay, but before you go, are you coming to the market on Sunday?'

Jill had forgotten the Christmas market.

'Yes, Emer, I'll be there. But I have to go now.'

'Missus, how much is this?' Once of the boys was standing in front of the counter holding up an outsized My Chemical Romance t-shirt in faded black.

'It's a euro.'

The boy fished a coin out of his pocket.

'Do you want a bag?'

No thanks, missus, I'll wear it now.'

He stripped off his school shirt and pulled on the t-shirt, much to the amusement of his guffawing pals.

They shoved and jostled their way out of the shop and Jill tried to digest what she had just heard from Emer. A vague plan was beginning to formulate in her head. She started to laugh.

Next day Jill was late back from lunch, delayed by the long queue in the post office. People posting parcels and filling in those damn customs forms. Brexit, she supposed.

'Sorry, Hannah, I seem to be always late.'

Hannah brushed the apology aside. She clearly had something important to say. 'You'll never guess what happened!'

'No, tell me, tell me.'

'Well, shortly after you left for lunch a man – your ex, I suppose – stormed into the shop. He was in a terrible state.'

Jill cringed. 'Oh God, go on.'

'Seems his partner found out he was playing the field, and...'

She paused.

'What?' Jill asked.

'She gave all his clothes away to a charity shop! Every stitch except what he had on him! Wanted to know if we had them!'

'What did you tell him?'

Hannah chuckled.

'I told him the truth.'

'The truth? What do you mean?'

'I said that the only donation of clothing we had yesterday was from someone who was moving abroad.'

Hannah laughed.

'Oh, yeah!' Jill said, fanning her face with her hands. 'What else? What else?'

Hannah was enjoying her role in the spotlight.

'When he asked to see them, I explained that the clothes were better quality than we normally get here, so we'd sold them on to our resellers.'

By now Jill was convulsed with laughter. She reached for Hannah's hand and gave it a warm squeeze.

'Oh, Hannah! You're so cool.'

'Support our sisters! That's what I say,' laughed Hannah. As an afterthought she added: 'Serves the bastard right!'

Jill stopped laughing. He, face creased with worry, she asked Hannah: 'Do you think that means I have to give up on the plan?'

'No, loveen,' said Hannah. 'You own the clothes now; you paid the staff price, and nobody can touch you. You just fire ahead with your plan and I hope it works out for you.'

Jill arrived at the Rowing Club early on Sunday morning.

It was a crisp, winter's day and the ripples on the river danced in the sunlight. Excitement was in the air as she walked into the old club house. Everywhere, people were bustling to get their stalls looking smart and inviting. Colourful rows of glittering fairy lights decorated the room. Mulled wine was bubbling gently on the stall nearest the door, right next to the aromatic hot chocolate. The various vendors were arranging candles, ornaments, crafts and gourmet foods to best effect. Delicious aromas wafted from the baked goods stall. The butcher was singing along to the music playing in the background, pretending to be Michael Bublé. I'm dreaming of a white Christmas.

It had taken Jill and Emer hours on Saturday evening to get the clothes priced and on hangers, so all they had to do in the morning was to set up the display. Emer's stall advertised itself as selling 'Pre-loved Men's and Women's Designer Clothing.' It was unusual to find men's clothing in the market and this novelty had begun to attract attention from some other traders, even before the arrival of the public. Bartering was encouraged among the traders. Before long, Jill had a Christmas cake, a pudding, a handmade crib, a beautiful garland and a voucher for a turkey. Emer agreed that the butcher would look dazzling over the festive period in his Ralph Lauren suit.

'That's Christmas sorted.' Jill said.

'Well, yes,' replied Emer, 'but hold on until you sell the clothes – you have cash flow problems, don't you?'

They need not have worried. Once the doors were opened the items were snapped up one by one – judging by the chat, mainly by women buying for the men in their lives. They oohed and aahed over the quality of the goods and the competitive prices.

'I think you'd still have sold them at double the price,' remarked Emer, as they prepared to break for lunch.

'But it's great as it is,' said Jill. 'Only one o'clock and there's hardly anything left. I've already cleared €400.'

On Christmas morning Billy and Jill were up before 8 – Billy to open his presents and Jill to put the turkey in the oven. The little apartment was transformed into a twinkling confection of fairy lights and decorations, and a respectable pile of wrapped presents lay beneath the Christmas tree.

'We have plenty of time to do everything before Emer and your cousins come over,' said Jill. 'You can help me with the vegetables after we've opened our presents and eaten breakfast.'

Billy would have agreed to anything at that moment. He began to investigate the pile. First out of the wrapping paper was an enormous Lego set. 'Oh Mum! Minecraft -The Dragon!' Nobody else in my class has this yet! Brilliant!'

Discarding the wrapping he moved onto another, softer parcel. 'Yay!' he shouted delightedly. 'How did Santa know I needed a new football strip? I didn't put it in the letter.'

The next parcel revealed a selection of art supplies – pencils, crayons, pens, little pots of poster paints, brushes and a large sketch pad. Billy danced up and down in delight. 'Now I can show Mr Flaherty how good an artist I am! Mum, isn't Santa great?'

He opened his last parcel and held up a green monogrammed sweater to show Jill. There were his initials – WS'- in gold letters. 'That stands for me!' he exclaimed. 'I love this! I'll wear it today!'

'Try it on,' Jill said, 'It looks as though it might be a bit big for you.' The child looked comical in the big sweater, but Jill couldn't spoil the moment by laughing. 'Not today, I'm afraid, but you're growing so fast, it won't be long before it's a perfect fit.'

Standing up to go into the kitchen, she turned to Billy. 'I'm really happy you like your presents, Billy.' She paused. 'You've been so good all year, and I always knew that Father Christmas would come to our rescue.'

'What do you mean our rescue, Mum?'

'Oh, never mind Billy.' She smiled at the boy. 'Let's have breakfast and start cooking for our guests. You can peel the sprouts!'

The Mizpah Ring

Sarah was spending another day clearing out the attic. With their eldest, James, away at university and their daughter, Jenny, on the cusp of leaving too, she and Ben were making tentative plans to downsize. But first, declutter! Everyone had a section of the attic for their stuff so at least the Barbie dolls, trainsets and Lego boxes were in some order. They could all go to charity.

But Ben's stuff?

Even though they had been married for years, his suitcases and backpacks, brought to the house when they first moved in, remained there. Untouched.

OK, I'll start with these. What a mess!

She rolled her sleeves up and started sorting items into a 'save' pile on her right and a 'trash' pile on her left. As the trash pile grew, so did Sarah's frustration with her hoarder husband. *Why is he saving all these books and papers?*

She was just thinking about having a break for lunch when she found the Tiffany ring-box.

Now, that's surprising? A ring-box among all this old junk? What's he hiding?

Her curiosity got the better of her. She opened the box.

'What on earth is this?' she said.

It was clearly an antique ring. A wide, gold circlet, with letters engraved on the outside. 'M-I-Z-P-A-H,' she read.

Inside, a single word: M-i-r-i-a-m.

Flustered, she took the ring closer to the attic window to get a better look. As hard as she tried, no logical explanation came to her mind for the appearance of the ring. Not for the first time, she felt overcome by a wave of insecurity. *How well do I really know my husband? What was Ben's life like before I met him?* Her stomach felt queasy. In dismay, she realised that her husband's past was still as mysterious as it was when they first met.

She busied herself absently for the rest of the afternoon, preparing dinner in a blur. After the meal was finished, when Ben had quaffed his customary glass of red – only the one, mind – he settled into his leather armchair to do the crossword.

Without preamble, she said:

'Ben, who is Miriam?'

He looked up from the newspaper.

'Miriam?'

'Do you know anyone named Miriam?'

Ben held his pen in mid-air. All thoughts of crossword solutions vanished. He closed the newspaper and put it to one side.

'Miriam?' he repeated, his voice puzzled.

'Yes! Miriam?'

'Why are you asking me?'

Sarah stared at him.

'What have you found out?' Ben asked. He rose to reach for the wine bottle. He retrieved his glass from the table and poured a generous measure.

'Found out?' said Sarah. She stood with her arms akimbo, realising that the next few minutes could determine the direction of their entire future.

Emboldened now, her voice quivered as she announced her discovery.

'A Tiffany box. A blue Tiffany box. Hidden in the attic.'

The silence in the room was broken only by the monotonous ticking of the mantlepiece clock.

With a sigh, Ben returned to his armchair, and took a long sip of wine.

'Is there anything you need to tell me, Ben?' Sarah asked, with a terrible sense of foreboding.

'Miriam,' he said. 'Yes, I know who Miriam was.'

Sarah's heart sank.

'Was?' she asked.

'It was a long time ago, Sarah. Miriam was my grandmother,' he said, quietly.

'Your grandmother?'

Sarah walked over to the sofa. She picked up a cushion and clutched it tightly. Then, she sat down.

'Granny in Leeds?'

'Miriam. My mother's birth mother. From Vienna.'

'Vienna? Oh, Ben. I never knew. You've never let me in.'

'I'm sorry, Sarah,' he said. 'I couldn't tell you. I had to keep it secret.'

Sarah responded gently: 'Ben, whatever it is, you can tell me. I love you. I have your back. Always!'

'I love you, Sarah. And I've been silent in deference to my mother's wishes, not because I wanted to keep anything from you.'

Ben's eyes focussed on the mantlepiece. The ticking clock hypnotised him. He imagined the streets of Vienna on the Night of Broken Glass. *Kristallnacht.*

'Ben? Ben? Talk to me, Ben!'

Sarah's voice brought him back to the present.

'Sarah, it was at the beginning of the war. Ruth, my mother, was born in Vienna. She came from a well-respected Jewish family. When she was five years old, in 1939, her parents Miriam and Max took the heroic step of enrolling her in the Kindertransport.'

'Kindertransport? I don't understand,' said Sarah. 'What was that?'

'It was a rescue effort that brought Jewish children to England in the lead-up to the Holocaust,' said Ben.

'Before she took her to the train station, Miriam fastened a gold ring on a chain around my mother's neck.'

'The ring in the attic,' whispered Sarah.

'A Mizpah ring,' said Ben. 'It has special significance in the Jewish tradition. It reminds the wearer that even when separated from their loved ones they are loved and watched over. The ring is supposed to bring good fortune and safe return.'

Ben and Sarah lapsed into silence. They each imagined what it must have been like. Crowds of people saying goodbye. Sadness because of the parting yet tinged with hope and optimism. A little girl clutching her possessions, following the other Jewish children into an uncertain future.

'It was the last time Ruth ever saw Miriam,' said Ben. 'My mother was placed with a Christian family in Leeds. They raised her as their own.'

'Did Ruth ever hear from her parents again?' asked Sarah, with tears in her eyes.

'Miriam wrote to her little girl over the next couple of years,' said Ben. 'The letters said nothing about the terrible times her family was going through in Vienna. The letters stopped coming when Miriam and Max were transported to Treblinka in 1943. They died without a trace.'

Sarah could no longer hide her emotions. She covered her face with her hands and sobbed.

Ben moved to the sofa and sat beside her. He put a comforting arm around her shoulder.

'When Ruth grew up and married my father,' said Ben, 'she moved to Ireland with him. Her Jewish heritage was never mentioned during my childhood. She wore the ring on a chain around her neck, all her life.'

'The poor, poor woman. It must have been horrible for her not knowing what happened to her parents.'

'I knew nothing about any of this until my mother passed away,' said Ben. 'She hadn't much to leave in her will, but she gave her papers and this box to me. There was a letter outlining her story and specific instructions about the ring. She wanted a generation to pass before any traces of her Jewish heritage resurfaced.'

'That is totally understandable,' said Sarah. 'No wonder she didn't feel safe in the world.' The Mizpah ring is the only memento I have of my grandmother's life and my own heritage,' said Ben. 'Jenny will have it before she goes to university, and I will tell her the whole story. I hope it will bring her good fortune and safe return.'

The Magic of Believing

It was the first day of the Christmas holidays. Conor, a lively 12-year-old with a head full of tangled curls, was playing football with his friends on the green outside their house. Their roars and shrieks could be heard from a mile away.

In the middle of the game, Conor felt something odd in his mouth. He reached in and pulled out his loose tooth. Holding it triumphantly, he yelled, 'Yay! Two euros!' The other boys, a mix of ages but all older than him, exchanged glances before bursting into laughter.

'Two euros? For a tooth?' one boy, Sean, said between chuckles. 'You're not serious, are you?'

Conor nodded enthusiastically. 'Yeah! The tooth fairy always leaves two euros under my pillow.'

The laughter intensified, and a few of the boys started to jeer. 'Conor still believes in the tooth fairy!' shouted another boy, Liam, his voice laced with mockery.

'Grow up, Conor,' Sean added, shaking his head. 'There's no such thing as a tooth fairy. That's just a story for babies.'

Their words hit Conor like a cold wave. His joy turned to embarrassment and hurt. He ran home, tears streaming down his face, feeling the sting of their ridicule.

Bursting into the kitchen, he found his mum. She was on one of her rare days off from the hospital. They happened less and less often since Dad left.

She looked up from unloading the dishwasher. 'Mum!' Conor shouted, his voice shaking. 'You lied to me!'

She turned, surprised by his outburst. Seeing his tearful eyes and the tooth in his hand, she looked puzzled. 'What do you mean, Conor?' she asked gently.

He confronted her, his hands trembling. 'And that letter! You wrote it, didn't you?' He was referring to a letter she had left under his pillow once, pretending to be from the tooth fairy, chiding him for not brushing his teeth enough.

Mum knelt down, trying to meet his eye. 'Yes, Conor, I wrote the letter. And... there's no tooth fairy,' she admitted, her voice filled with regret.

'Why did you lie to me?' he demanded.

She tried to explain, her voice quivering. 'It wasn't a lie, love. It was a bit of magic, a story to make childhood more special.'

'But I believed in it! You made me look stupid!' Conor wiped his eyes, feeling angry and foolish.

'I'm sorry, Conor. I never meant to make you look stupid,' she said, her eyes brimming with tears.

He whispered, barely audible, 'I wish you hadn't.'

She watched him struggle with a dawning realization.

His emotions boiled over. 'I suppose next you'll tell me you're Santa too?'

Mum's heart sank further. 'Oh Conor,' she began softly, 'Santa Claus is a wonderful story, a

The Magic of Believing

beautiful tradition... but he's not real, not in the way you think.'

'Not real?' Conor repeated, his world upending. 'What are you saying? No Dad; no tooth fairy; and now, no Santa?'

'Parents tell these stories to make Christmas special. But it's really us. We put the presents under the tree,' she explained.

'So, all of it... the whiskey and Christmas cake, the carrot... it's all just... a lie?' he asked, struggling now.

'No, not a lie,' she insisted gently. 'It's a story we share, a way to celebrate the spirit of giving and love.'

'Why didn't you just tell me?' he asked, not knowing whether to be sad or angry.

'We wanted to give you the joy of believing in something magical,' she said softly.

'Mum, it's not just about believing in Santa. It's about... about trusting what you say,' Conor, near to tears, replied.

'I'm so sorry, Conor. I never wanted to hurt you or betray your trust.'

'I suppose... I'll just have to grow up, then,' he shouted.

Conor stormed out of the kitchen, slamming the door behind him. He could sense Mum's heartbreak in the silence that followed.

He pounded up the stairs, his emotions raw and overwhelming. He banged around his room in a storm of anger and disappointment. Then, he came back down, holding a PlayStation console.

'This! This never worked properly!' he yelled at Mum. 'You said we couldn't send it back to the

North Pole. Now you can just go and exchange it for one that works!'

Mum, trying to stay calm, replied, 'I can try to fix it, Conor. Or we can see about getting it exchanged.'

'You said Santa's elves made it, but they didn't, did they? It's just a broken game from a shop!' His voice was thick with anger and betrayal.

'I'm sorry, Conor. I know this is hard for you. I really meant to get you another one but there's been so much going on,' she said, her own emotions swirling.

He looked at the console, then back at her. He placed the console on the kitchen table, his shoulders slumping. He felt awful for shouting. He knew she was just as upset as he was. He knew she had to work so hard to keep everything together for him and his brothers.

'I just want things to be the way they used to be, Mum,' Conor said quietly.

Later, Mum asked him to go for a walk with her.

'If you want to talk about that Santa stuff, forget it. I'm okay now,' he said.

Mum sighed, looking into his upset eyes. 'Still, we need to talk,' she insisted.

As they strolled towards the green, Mum began.

'Conor, when you asked, 'Are you Santa?' that was a good question; and the answer is no, I'm not Santa. There isn't just a single Santa.'

Conor listened, the crisp air around them seeming to stand still.

'I fill your stockings with presents and wrap the gifts under the tree, just like my mum did for me, and her mum before her,' she continued. 'And yes, your dad used to be part of it too, when he was here.'

The path beneath their feet crunched with every step.

'One day, you might do the same for your children. And you'll love seeing their joy on Christmas morning. But doing it doesn't make you Santa.'

Mum paused. 'Santa is more than one single person. He's a team of people, mums, and dads, all over the world. Santa's work is about teaching children to believe in something they can't see or touch. It's a big, important job.'

Her words hung in the air, confusing Conor.

They walked in silence for a bit, the sounds of the neighbourhood distant and muffled.

'Now you know Santa's secret. When we are young, he fills our hearts with joy. As we get older, we help him carry on the tradition. People like your dad and me, and now, you.'

Mum looked at him, her eyes full of love. 'We're on Santa's team, Conor. We help with his impossible job. Santa is love and magic. He's hope and happiness.'

Conor felt a lump in his throat as her words sank in.

'So, no, I'm not Santa,' Mum concluded. 'But I'm part of what he represents. And now, so are you.'

After a pause, Mum spoke again. 'Conor, I have a big job for you tomorrow. Will you come into work with me?'

'What for?' Conor asked.

'We're having a Christmas party for the children on the ward. We have presents for all of them,' Mum explained with a hopeful smile. 'Santa is coming to visit and I'd love you to be his helper.'

His expression changed from curiosity to surprise. 'Me? Helping Santa?'

'Yes, you,' Mum said warmly. These kids need the spirit of Santa, more than most of us. They could do with some hope and joy.'

'What would I need to do?' Conor inquired.

'Dress up, help hand out presents, talk to the kids a bit, make them smile,' Mum said. 'Bring a little bit of happiness to the ones who might be feeling sad.'

'I suppose... that's what Santa's really about, isn't it? Making people happy?'

Mum smiled. 'Exactly, Conor. And by being there, by giving some of your time and care, you're keeping Santa's work going. You're keeping hope alive for the sick children.'

Conor stood a bit taller. 'Okay, Mum. I'll do it. I'll be Santa's helper.'

Mum reached out, squeezing his hand gently. 'I'm proud of you, Conor. You're going to make those children very happy.'

Mary Rose Tobin

Winner of the 2023 Siarscéal Hanna Greally International Short Story Competition

The Life and Times of Jimmy Mullins

The Life and Times of Jimmy Mullins

I was sitting in the Control Room when the phone jangled, breaking my reverie. The authoritative voice on the other end belonged to the Director-General.

'We need to admit a new boy from the courts.'

'We're at full capacity,' I replied, frustration creeping into my voice.

'You'll need to make space,' he retorted. 'Don't sigh down the phone at me. Send somebody home.'

'But there's nobody ready!' I bleated.

'That's too bad. You're in charge while I'm not there. These are the kinds of decisions you need to get used to making.'

He hung up.

I've worked at St Dermot's Secure School as Deputy Director, since it opened in March. My job? To provide a semblance of structure, discipline, and, if possible, a touch of compassion to the thirty teenage boys under our care at any given time. Navigating a ship through a never-ending storm.

It had been a long day so far, and I didn't need this. I needed to focus on the Christmas Mass and Dinner.

For the boys of St Dermot's, Christmas was a big deal. Minding our charges was tough at the best of times but keeping their spirits up over the festive season was particularly hard.

'Will I be getting out for Christmas?' was the constant chorus. When the answer was 'No', even the most hardened boys would lash out, kicking lockers and spewing strings of curses. Dublin mothers insisted that their sons had special Christmas clothes; as one of them put it, they had to be 'new from the skin out'. If a boy didn't have permission to go shopping with his mother, she somehow managed to bring his new outfit to the school.

We rarely saw the fathers.

The boys did their utmost to push the staff to their limits. In school they threw pencil cases, overturned desks, and tossed books to the floor. Any staff member who tried to engage in a positive way had their words thrown back, laced with expletives. In the dining room, the housekeeping staff were driven to despair with food smeared on walls and trays discarded carelessly.

Yet, every Saturday, without fail, the visiting room was full. Mothers in worn-out coats disembarked from old buses or walked long distances, carrying special treats and hope in their eyes. They hugged their sons, ignoring the stares and whispers, their love evident and unwavering.

The air in the assembly hall, today doubling as a chapel, was thick with anticipation. The smell of pine needles and the sweet scent of the candles burning on the altar mingled with the smell of the boys' freshly laundered clothes. The sound of their shuffling feet and the occasional whisper of a joke filled the room. The warmth was palpable; light from the candles and the Christmas tree shimmered in the boys' eyes.

The priest stepped forward, raising his hands in a gesture of peace. As the first notes of the hymn began, the boys joined in, filling the room with a resonance that was powerful and unexpected. Their voices wavered at times, but the strength of their collective spirit was undeniable.

Glancing around the room, my eyes met those of a woman with tear-streaked cheeks. She clutched a handkerchief tightly, her gaze fixed on one of the singing boys. The handmade jumper and the carefully wrapped gifts at his feet spoke of a mother's love, a desperate wish for her son to feel the joy of Christmas, even in these circumstances. I fought back my own tears.

The priest nodded, and one of the boys, Jimmy, approached the altar. He clutched a piece of paper in his hand. Taking a deep breath, he began, 'A letter from St Paul to the C-C-Co...' He paused, collecting himself. Whispers of encouragement drifted from the back. With a determined look, he tried again.

'A letter from St Paul to the C-C-Co-Coalminers.'

The room was silent for a heartbeat, then a burst of spontaneous applause erupted. Boys cheered, some shouting words of encouragement, others clapping him on the back. The pride in his effort was spontaneous, their collective support evident.

As Jimmy shuffled back to his chair, I caught his eye.

'Well done,' I mouthed.

***

The Director-General's phone call had left me in an invidious position. When dinner ended, I made my way back to the Control Room, situated between the admin block and the secure unit. A reinforced glass window provided a clear view into the boys' quarters. On a central desk, radios and walkie-talkies stood ready in their chargers, their soft beeps intermittently breaking the silence. Alongside, a pegboard held an array of labelled keys, each representing a door or gate within the school. The polished floor reflected the room's overhead lights, while CCTV monitors on the wall continuously showed various parts of the school. It was the heartbeat of the institution, a blend of vigilance and order.

My mind turned to Jimmy. Though far from ready to go home, he seemed like the best option. He was a meek boy, well behaved, and out of place here. Had life dealt him a different hand, he might have been at home with his family now, preparing for Christmas with his brothers and sisters.

I contacted Tony, the social worker, urgency evident in my voice. Retrieving Jimmy's file, I dialled his home number, but the line echoed with a monotonous buzz. I quickly reread his admission report to refresh myself on the details. It was a catalogue of deprivation and abuse. His mother, dealing with addiction and personal demons, would sometimes disappear for days, leaving Jimmy and his siblings to fend for themselves. In his early days at the school he had flinched at the slightest touch, his eyes always darting around as if expecting danger from every corner. When he first arrived, having been convicted of a minor offense, I talked to him about it. I asked, 'Jimmy, why are you here? What did you do?' He replied, 'Well, me charge sheet says I was 'interfering with the magnificent.' I remembered this as I flicked through his file and saw the actual charge written on the sheet – 'interfering with the mechanism of a mechanically propelled vehicle.' I couldn't help smiling.

Despite his past, Jimmy had shown remarkable resilience. Over the last few months, he had begun to find his place, building trust with a few of the staff and forming hesitant friendships with some of the boys. It was heart breaking to even consider sending him back to the environment he'd so narrowly escaped.

As the Director-General's words echoed in my mind, I felt torn. The pragmatic part of me recognised the logistical challenge; we couldn't take in another boy without making space. But my heart resisted. These weren't just numbers; they were lives, each with its own story and potential. Who was I to be playing God, choosing one over the other?

Looking at the CCTV screens, I watched as Jimmy laughed at something one of the other boys said, his smile a brief moment of genuine happiness amidst the institutional gloom. The weight of my impending decision pressed down on me even more.

I walked down to the common room. The warm glow of the TV lit the area. Jimmy was engrossed in a snooker match.

'Jimmy,' I beckoned, voice softer than intended. 'You're heading home.'

His face lit up, eyes wide.

'Really? Now?'

There was a quiver of excitement in his voice.

We moved into the bedroom corridor. I unlocked his door and together we gathered his belongings. The familiar scent of his room, the muted colours of his clothes, the soft shuffle as we packed – every sensation amplified, a stark reminder of the impending void.

Tony waited by the van, its engine murmuring softly. As I said goodbye to Jimmy there was a catch in my voice. 'Stay out of trouble,' I whispered.

'I...I...I'll do me best,' he promised.

Later, as darkness settled, Tony returned, his face etched with exhaustion. He began recounting the evening's events. When they reached Jimmy's home, the curtains were drawn, and an eerie silence hung in the air. After what seemed like an eternity, a neighbour peeked out, her face creased with irritation. 'She's in the pub,' the woman shouted, pointing an accusing finger in the direction of O'Reilly's. Tony nodded, thanking her, and took the boy to look for his mother.

The pub was noisy, dimly lit, and reeked of stale beer. They made their way through the crowd, searching for Mrs Mullins. When they finally found her, she was hunched over a table, a drink in her hand, surrounded by raucous friends.

There were no tears of joy, no tight embraces. As Jimmy approached, she looked up, her expression a complex mixture of surprise, guilt, and pain. Her eyes barely recognised her son. Jimmy's hopeful gaze met hers, searching for a hint of affection. Her indifference, exaggerated by her intoxicated state, wounded him. The boy could barely hold back the tears.

'But I had to leave him there.' Tony went on. 'I bought him a glass of orange. What else could I do?'

***

The days that followed were a whirlwind of Christmas preparations. I found solace in the familiar traditions – wrapping presents, decorating the tree, and baking treats that filled the air with delightful aromas. The shimmering lights and cheerful carols almost managed to push the memory of the school and the boys to the back of my mind.

Having some long-anticipated leave, I decided to travel up to my parents' house in the countryside. It was a welcome break, a place where the cacophony of the city was replaced by the soft whisper of wind through the trees and the crackling of the log fire. For the first time in months, I felt genuinely relaxed, the weight of responsibility temporarily lifted. I lost hours sitting by the window, watching snowflakes dance in the winter air and feeling grateful for the homeliness and love that surrounded me.

But this peace was short-lived. One evening, while enjoying a glass of wine and browsing through a local newspaper, a headline caught my eye and cut through my festive haze. The familiar warmth drained away, replaced by a chilling realisation that the world outside was far from the idyllic scene in which I had lost myself.

> **Teen Tragedy**
> **Boy Perishes in Blaze, Companion Narrowly Survives**
> In a horrifying accident that has sent shockwaves through the city, a 14-year-old boy named as Jimmy Mullins became the victim of a catastrophic blaze that reduced an abandoned building to ashes last night.

The article painted a grim picture. Two runaways frequented an abandoned building with a few other local kids. It became their hideaway – a place where they'd share stolen cigarettes, recount tales of their escapades, talk and dream. The building was decrepit but offered a semblance of shelter and camaraderie.

The weather turned particularly bitter one evening. With nowhere else to turn, Jimmy and his friend decided to light a small fire to keep themselves warm. They believed they had things under control. They weren't to know the house had been used as a makeshift car-repair shop. The vicinity was laden with old rags, empty petrol containers, oil cans and other flammable debris. Within minutes, the entire place was alight. The other boy managed a harrowing escape, but Jimmy was tragically trapped.

My stomach lurched. Memories of that recent Christmas Mass flooded back. I pictured Jimmy's face, innocent and vulnerable, stammering at the scripture reading. The laughing eyes from the CCTV screen haunted my mind.

Christmas cheer was replaced by a heavy silence. Festive lights appeared dimmer; their twinkling overshadowed by a profound sense of loss. Overcome with a potent cocktail of guilt, despair, and accountability, I drained my wine glass and reflexively reached for another bottle.

About the Author

Mary Rose Tobin was born and raised in Galway. She moved to Dublin to embark on a fulfilling career in the public sector. Upon retiring, she returned to the scenic village of Barna. She continues to work with the Mental Health Commission on a part-time basis, underscoring her dedication to fostering a healthy community.

Mary Rose sings with the Galway Choral Association and is also an accomplished writer. As a founding member of Write-on, she has contributed to the Anthologies since 2019. Her writings, much like her life, blend her love for family and community, her passion for public service, and her dedication to mental health. She cherishes her daily walks by the sea. This simple ritual not only attests to her love for nature, but also to her belief in the importance of mental well-being, reflecting the calm and tranquillity she brings to her work.

'We are all apprentices in a craft where no one ever becomes a master.'

Ernest Hemingway, *The Wild*

Printed in Great Britain
by Amazon